KILL JILL

(A Love Story)

John Locke

TELEMACHUS PRESS

The characters and events in this book are fictitious. Any similarity to real persons, living or dead, is coincidental and not intended by the author.

KILL JILL

Cover Designed by: Telemachus Press, LLC
Copyright © Shutterstock/61556335

Visit the author's website:
http://www.donovancreed.com

Published by: Telemachus Press, LLC
http://www.telemachuspress.com

ISBN: 978-1-939337-37-5 (eBook)
ISBN: 978-1-939337-38-2 (EPUB)
ISBN: 978-1-939337-39-9 (Paperback)

Printed in the United States of America
10   9   8   7   6   5   4   3   2   1

KILL JILL

Part One:
NEW GIRL IN TOWN

Chapter 1

Willow Lake, Arkansas.
7:55 a.m.

The heavy fog that holds Willow Lake hostage most mornings usually burns off around eight-thirty. Since that's a half-hour away, Frank the cab driver relies on the strident electronic voice of his GPS navigation system that directs him to follow Route 53 North for another mile. He does so, then turns left on Front Street, right on Trimble, and from there it's two blocks to Fillmore's Grocery and Dry Goods Store. He pulls into the empty parking lot, selects a space, and cuts the engine.

A moment later, the back door opens.

Frank's lone passenger, a lady, slides out.

Mavis Fillmore peers out her store window and becomes the first person in Willow Lake to get a look at the newcomer. She mentally appraises the woman as thirty, extremely attractive, citified, shapely. She's also wearing clothes that, while stylish, appear to be covered with grass and soot stains. As if she slept in them last night, in a field, after cleaning a fireplace. Her hair's unkempt. She's not carrying a purse. When she turns to say something to the cab driver, Mavis notices a thick envelope poking out the back pocket of her skin-tight jeans.

"New customer," Mavis sniffs.

Her husband, Ziff, looks up from his paper and says, "*This* time of year?"

"Pulled up just now. In a *cab*, no less."

"Man or woman?"

Mavis gives him a stern look and says, "Let me put it this way. I catch you starin' at her ass or boobs you'll have to come up with a new way to piss."

Chapter 2

When the front door opens, Ziff Fillmore jumps to his feet.

"Can I help you, ma'am?"

"Thanks, I m good," the lady says, pulling a shopping cart from the rack.

"Season's over," Mavis says. "What brings you to town?"

The lady pushes her cart down the first aisle, pretending not to hear. Fifteen minutes later, at the checkout register, she asks, "Can you tell me where I might find a stepladder?"

Mavis frowns. "Why the hell do you need a stepladder?"

"Excuse me?"

"Whose cabin did you rent?"

The lady says nothing.

Mavis says, "You pulled up in a cab."

"So?"

Mavis points at the purse in the lady's cart. "Ours ain't as fancy as you're probably used to."

"This one will suit me just fine."

"What happened to you?"

The lady looks down at her soiled tunic top and jeans. "I'd rather not talk about it. Can you just scan my items?"

Mavis coughs out an ugly laugh. "*Scan* them?"

"Sorry. I mean, ring them up."

Mavis frowns, but starts ringing up the items as the lady places them on the counter. She stares at each with mounting suspicion. Toothpaste? Toothbrush? Shampoo? *Lipstick? Hairbrush?* These are basic items a woman should already have among her possessions.

"I can't stand it any longer," Mavis says.

"What's wrong?"

"We don't *have* cabs in Willow Lake."

"So?"

"So you ain't from around here. And another thing: I bet you ain't laid eyes on your cabin yet, but somehow you already know you need a *stepladder?*"

"I'm sorry," the lady says. "I'm not used to these types of questions from total strangers. Let's just forget about the stepladder."

Ziff says, "Clyde Jones owns the hardware store on Second Street. He opens around eight-thirty, which is in about..." He checks his watch. "Ten minutes. You'll find a suitable stepladder there, I expect. By the way, I'm Ziff. This here's Mavis. She's my wife. What I mean is, we're married."

Mavis frowns at her husband's clumsy attempt at conversation with a woman who, despite her current state of disarray, is far and away the sexiest to ever step foot in Willow Lake.

"I'm Emma Wilson. Nice to meet you both." She reaches into her cart and places the last few items on the counter.

4

Mavis puts her hands on her ample hips and says, "Well?"

"Well, what?"

"Where you from, Emma?"

"Out of town."

"Really? Out of town? Well so's the Pope and Derby Pie. Which cabin did you rent?"

"I'm not renting. But from what I understand, it's a lake house."

"Who owns it?"

"My fiancé."

Mavis and Ziff do a double-take. Mavis says, "Who the hell's your fiancé?"

Emma says, 'I don't wish to be rude. I realize whenever a new asshole enters the dog pound there's going to be a certain amount of sniffing. But this is ridiculous. Can you just ring up my purchases and let me be on my way?"

Mavis starts puffing up as if to launch a tirade, but is interrupted by the sudden, soundless appearance of Emma's taxi driver. Mavis instantly appraises him as she does all strangers, and finds him much larger and less friendly than any cab drivers she's ever seen.

"Is there a problem here?" he says.

Emma says, 'I'm not sure."

A look of concern crosses Mavis's face. She starts to say something, changes her mind. Rings up Emma's items, and Ziff scrambles to bag them.

"One sixty-three seventy-two," Mavis says.

Emma hands her two crisp one-hundred-dollar bills.

Mavis frowns, holds them up to the light, and studies them like a rabbinical student studies the Talmud.

After what seems an extraordinary amount of time, she says, "You got an ID?"

Emma fishes her driver's license from her front left pocket, hands it to Mavis.

After a minute she says, "I figured you for thirty. I was right."

She hands back Emma's ID, puts the bills in the register, counts out the change. Says, "Somethin' ain't right here."

Emma turns, walks toward the entrance. Cabbie picks up the grocery bags, follows her out the door.

"I'll have my answers!" Mavis hollers.

Chapter 3

Ziff says, "You were pretty rude just now."

"And you were fallin' all over yourself tryin' to be helpful."

"The lady wants a stepladder. What's the big deal?"

"I saw how you looked at her. It'll take her two hours in the shower to scrub your eyes off her tits."

"You're crazy."

"You think? We just been through a triple homicide, don't forget."

"What're you talking about?"

"Lottie Sikes."

"Lottie was local. She killed herself and two cats. That hardly qualifies as a triple homicide."

"Oh yeah? Well, trust no one, that's my motto. Fiancé my ass! Go outside and check the license plate. I'll wager five dollars it's an out-of-stater."

Ziff shakes his head, but walks outside, stands on the porch, pretends to wave goodbye. Watches the cab back up, drive away. Notes the license plate. Continues standing there long after she's gone. Day-dreaming what it would be like to see Emma Wilson naked.

To touch her.

To wake up beside her, just once.

From inside, Mavis yells, "Put your dick back in your pants!"

His dick *is* in his pants.

But he wishes it wasn't.

He sighs, enters the store. "Plates are from Tennessee."

"I told you so," Mavis says.

"That's somethin' I don't hear often enough."

"Call Ellwood, she says."

"Why?"

"Tell him drive to the hardware store, and be quick about it. Tell him to follow that cab till he finds out which lake house Little Miss Dirty Britches is stayin' in."

"Why do you care?"

"Right. Just stand there and tell me you ain't the least bit curious about a woman who comes in here lookin' like she rolled through two miles of hen shit, carryin' hundred dollar bills, with no purse, no wallet, and gets driven around by a Mafia cab driver who practically threatened to kill us."

"*Kill* us?"

"Call Ellwood."

Ziff calls their son.

Thirty minutes later, the store phone rings. Mavis checks the caller ID before answering.

"Well?" she says.

"You didn't tell me she was a movie star."

"Movie star?"

"Well, she's got the looks for it."

"But she's not, is she? Far as you know?"

"No. I just mean she's hot."

"Where's she stayin'?"

"That dog guy's place."

"*Dog* guy? What the hell are you talkin' about, Ellwood?"

"The guy that's never here. Can't think of his name. But you know him. The guy all the women swoon over? The one named like a breed of dog."

Mavis thinks a minute. "Jack Russell?"

"Yeah. But he weren't with her."

"You watched them unload the cab?"

"Uh huh."

"How much luggage did she have?"

"Three grocery bags and a stepladder."

"That's *it?*"

"Uh huh."

"You sayin' she had *no* suitcase?"

"Right."

"No carry bag?"

"Not that I could see."

"Somethin' definitely ain't right about all this."

"For Jack Russell, it is," Ellwood says. "Lucky bastard."

"Watch your tongue, young man!" Mavis snaps.

She shakes her head. That's all this town needs after what it's been through, with the triple homicide and all. A pretty, single woman to get the men all hot and bothered, thinkin' how their own wives and girlfriends suddenly don't measure up. In an hour Miss Emma Wilson will be all cleaned up. By ten the clothing stores at the Jessup Mall will be open. She'll have the big cab driver take her there to buy a new wardrobe. By noon the whole town will be talkin' about the pretty little thing who's fuckin' Jack Russell, the building contractor from St. Louis, who shows up three times a year for maybe two weeks at a time. Jack's handsome enough to get anyone he wants, but this one's clearly usin' him for the house key. And who carries hundred-dollar bills around in their jeans' pockets these days, aside from drug dealers and prostitutes?

That's what Mavis wants to know.

Chapter 4

"She's probably in there right now, takin' a shower," Ellwood says.

"Probably scrubbin' her body with a facecloth full of sweet-smellin' soap," says his friend, Cobb, on speaker phone.

Ellwood sips his coffee while keeping an eye on the front door of Jack Russell's place. It's a cool morning, but not so cold he can't keep the window open on his F150. He'd like to describe Emma's body, but the front door suddenly opens.

"Cab driver's comin' out," Ellwood says.

"How long was he in there?"

"Fifteen minutes, give or take."

"You think he did her?"

"Of course not! He's a fuckin' *cab* driver! And she's engaged."

"I'd engage her, but not with a ring," Cobb says.

The big man stands on the porch, checks his watch, then starts walking down the road.

"What's he doin' now?" Cobb says.

"Takin' a walk."

"Did he see you?"

"Nah. I'm at the watch point."

"Well, hell buddy, go on in there and get you some!"

"Nothin' I'd like more.

"What's her name?"

"Emma Wilson."

"She sounds fat."

"Oh, fuck you, Cobb!" He pauses, then says, "You know how their nipples get hard in the shower?"

"Tilly Chesapeake had them kind of nipples. They'd pop out so long and hard you could hang clothes on 'em."

"That must've come in handy for Tilly at the laundromat. Whatever become of her?"

"I heard she moved to Fordyce and got her tit caught in a wringer."

They laugh.

"You know what I think?" Ellwood says.

"What's that?"

"A woman like Emma Wilson would never piss in the shower."

"A 'course she would!" Cobb says. "I don't care how pretty she is. They all piss in the shower when they're alone."

"Not Emma."

"She's probably pissin' in there right now. Whoa! Did you hear that?"

"What?"

"I think she just farted!"

"Shut up, Cobb!"

"Pissin' and fartin' is biological functions. All women'll do them things when they're alone."

Ellwood scrunches his face up. "How would *you* know what they do if they only do it when they're alone?"

"Cold, hard facts, Ellwood. You can look 'em up if you want."

"Where?"

"The internet is full of statistical data about this shit. Not to mention all them women's magazines."

"Like the ones *you* read?"

They laugh.

Ellwood says, "Well, I can promise you Emma Wilson don't do none of them things. Wait till you lay eyes on her."

"Maybe I'll lay some pipe, instead."

"Out of your league, Cobb. And that's a biological fact of chemistry."

"She can't be *that* special."

"She is. And movie star pretty. Plus, there's somethin' in the way she carries herself, you know?"

"You are so full of shit. She's probably butt-ugly, and you're still drunk from last night."

"You've seen Jack Russell," Ellwood says.

"So?"

"You think he'd be engaged to a butt-ugly woman?"

"How the fuck would I know? He's like thirty-five, right? The dude's nearly twice our age!"

They go quiet a minute. Then Cobb says, "You plannin' to follow her all day?"

"Got nothin' better to do."

"Must be nice. Me? I gotta go. Fence won't build itself. Let me know what happens."

"Count on it."

They hang up and Ellwood's ear suddenly hurts like hell.

Chapter 5

"This ear tissue," the cabbie says, applying more pressure, "Is very delicate. You'd be amazed how much damage I can do with just my thumb and forefinger."

"Wh-what do you *want?*" Ellwood gasps.

"Funny, I was about to ask *you* the same question!"

"Wh-what do you m-mean?"

"You followed us here from the store. You've been parked here all this time, spying. Now you're waiting for something. I ask myself what're the chances you do this every day? Go to the hardware store, park up here off-road, on a hill, under tree cover, spy on Jack Russell's lake house. And you know what I come up with? Never. You never do this. Except I see tire tracks here, and a clearing. As if maybe you don't do this every day, but you've done it before. What's your name?"

"Ellwood. *Oww!*"

"Your *full* name, asswipe!"

"*Fillmore!* Jeez! Ellwood *Fillmore.*"

"Like the grocery store?"

"My p-parents."

"You've been here before, haven't you, Ellwood?"

"Y-Yes. Can you let go of me? I-I can't feel my ear!"

"Amazing how painful that is. Not sure why."

The cabbie's cell phone rings. He releases Ellwood's ear, checks his phone, puts it back in his pocket. Says, "Normally, I'd kill you. But I got enough shit in my life right now. Don't need the aggravation. I assume your mother's responsible for this?"

"Huh?"

"Did your mother tell you to spy on Emma?"

"Uh huh."

"Why?"

"Why do you think? She's a nosy bitch!"

The cabbie laughs. "Well said. But you love her? Or just don't want to be on her bad side."

"Both."

"How long you been spying on Jack Russell's place?"

"Never. I mean, there's trails all around here. Me and my friends come up here all the time."

"Smoke dope? Party? Have sex?"

"Stuff like that."

"Just a coincidence you've got a perfect view of Jack's place?"

"Trails give us a perfect view of *all* the rentals. Cabins, lake houses..."

"Who else comes up here? You know, to hang out."

"Uh...you mean, what, you want names? *Everyone* comes up here to hang out. I'd have to name—*Ow!* Aw, shit! Stop! That hurts like *hell!*"

"You know what I think? I think you and your friends drive up here to park your trucks, but you don't party up here on the hill. You break into the empty houses and cabins."

"No sir!"

"His house has been vandalized."

"*What?*"

"Completely cleaned out. Everything gone. Electronics, booze, fishing rods. All gone."

"That's not true! The booze, maybe, but—"

The cabbie smiles. "Gotcha!"

"Shit."

He releases Ellwood's ear for the second time. "Want to talk about it?"

"Not really."

"I'm impressed with the girls you bring. Or women, possibly."

"What do you mean?"

"They tidy up nicely after the parties."

Ellwood says nothing.

Cabbie says, "I'm a reasonable guy. I'll give you a reasonable choice. You can tell me the truth right now, or we can have a chat with the sheriff."

"Sheriff?"

"Someone knocked the glass panel out the back door and taped it shut to keep the bugs out. Beyond that, the booze is gone. None of that bothers me. Hell, I don't even know this guy, Jack Russell. But I'll tell you what I do know. You and your buddies thought it would be fun to put holes in Russell's condoms. See which local woman winds up pregnant. You think the sheriff might want to express an opinion on that?"

17

Ellwood pauses. "What do you want?"

"Two favors."

"What?"

"Get that window fixed before we get back from the mall."

"*What?*"

"You'll have about three hours."

"I didn't even *do* it! I just show up, man."

"Don't fuck with me, son, or I'll turn your nut sack into a coin purse. I want that window fixed before I get back. I don't care how you make it happen. Are we clear?"

"Yes, sir."

They look at each other a minute, then Ellwood says, "What's the second thing?"

"Stay away."

"From her?"

"The house."

"Why?"

"Because Jack Russell will be here soon, and he's not going to be happy to hear you've been breaking into his place."

"You're gonna tell him?"

"I'll decide after I see if the window's fixed."

Ellwood pauses. Then says, "Who *is* she?"

"I never met her before last night. But I like her. And as long as I'm in a position to help keep her safe, I will."

Chapter 6

2:50 p.m.

"Am I the first to visit you?" Milly Reston says.

"Yes. And I'm happy to meet you."

"You and Jack are engaged?"

"We are."

Milly makes a sour face. "When a woman moves in with a man, there's not much incentive for marriage. From the man's point of view, I mean."

"I'll keep that in mind," Emma says.

They're at the kitchen table, drinking tea. The broccoli-cheese casserole Milly brought for Emma's dinner is cooling on the counter, too hot for the fridge.

"Our water's fine, you know," Milly says, eyeing the stack of bottled waters on the floor, by the hallway.

"It's a habit, I suppose."

"A costly one, if you ask me."

Emma shrugs.

Milly says, "Want me to help put the canned goods in the cupboard?"

"No, thanks."

"Why not?"

"It'll give me something to do later on."

"When's Jack comin'?"

"I'm not sure."

"I don't mean the exact day. But later in the week? *Next* week?"

"I really don't know."

"You mean he might not show up for *weeks*?"

"He might not."

"*Months*?"

Emma shrugs. "Jack's traveling, trying to sell his business. He'll come when he can."

"He just what, gave you his *key*? Said move in, wait till he could join you?"

"That's right."

"He must really love you to trust you with his place." She lets her eyes roam the room a minute, then whispers, "Have you gone through his *things* yet?"

"What do you mean?"

"You know...snoop!"

"No, of *course* not!"

"Really?" Milly says. "Because *I* would! I'd do it in a *heartbeat*! I'd open every door, read every receipt, learn everything I possibly could about the man."

"Why?"

"*Why?* Hell girl, because you're here and he's not! Because you're plannin' to *marry* him! Because you'll never have a better chance to learn his *secrets!* Why are you lookin' at me like that? Don't tell me you're not curious!"

"Sorry. I'm not."

"Not even the teeniest, smallest amount?"

"Not even."

"*Seriously,* Emma?"

Emma shrugs.

Milly glances around the room again. "I wouldn't be able to sleep! Not till I'd searched every nook and cranny. Every can in the cupboard. Every box in the attic. Every loose floor board under the carpet. The ice trays. The lining of his jackets and bedspreads. I'd search day and night till I found them all."

"Found what?"

"His *hiding places*, silly! All men have them. And it's our job to find out where they are. And what they're hidin' in them. And why. Are you okay, hon? You're lookin' at me funny again. Like you ate a bug or somethin'."

"I'm speechless," Emma says.

"Well, you can thank me later by tellin' me what you found. And if you want, I'll be glad to help. All you need do is ask."

"Thanks for the offer."

"Don't mention it." She lowers her voice and says, "How much of Jack's past has he shared?"

"Enough to get me here."

Milly nods. Then bites the corner of her lip and says, "Has he mentioned Abbie Rhodes?"

"Not that I recall. Why?"

"Just a town rumor. Take it with a grain of salt."

"Okay."

"I'll say the secret if you want."

"No, that's okay."

"If it was me, I'd want to know."

Emma says nothing.

Milly frowns. "I should tell you."

"I'd rather you didn't. But what can you tell me about the sheriff?"

Milly raises an eyebrow. "You heard about him and Linda Craig?"

"Not yet."

"Well!" she says. "You didn't hear it from me, okay?"

"Okay."

"Sheriff Cox and Linda dated in high school. He went to Arkansas State, she went to Southern Miss, married a football player. After her divorce last year, she moved back to town. Sheriff's a married man, but word around town is he's met her out by Palmer Lake at night."

"Has anyone seen them together?"

"Ronny Tucker saw their cars together once. Says he slowed down enough to see no one's head was higher up than the windows, if you catch my drift."

Emma laughs.

Milly says, "Now that we've got that one out of the way, let me tell you what they're sayin' about Abbie and Jack."

"Another time, perhaps."

Milly sighs. "Very well. But this whole business about movin' in with the man?"

"Yes?"

"Soon you'll pass the point of no return. You understand?"

"Not really."

"I mean, once he moves in, it's too late. You can't undo what's already done."

"Well, in this case, I'm the one who's moving in."

A look of confusion crosses Milly's face.

Emma says, "I'm not interested in marrying Jack. Not immediately, anyway."

Milly's eyes widen. "You're not interested in marrying Jack *Russell?*"

"Not immediately."

"Blond-haired, blue-eyed, perfectly chiseled, dazzling-smiled Jack *Russell?* Did I mention friendly, funny, *wealthy* Jack Russell?"

"Is this really such a shock for you to hear?"

"If you're telling the *truth*, it is. If you're telling the truth, it's *beyond* shock, it's *insane!* It's...it's...*unfathomable!*"

"Why?"

"Every woman in the county has a thing for Jack. You need to tie him up, girl! Aren't you afraid you're gonna *lose* him?"

"Nope."

Milly shakes her head. "None of this makes a lick of sense."

"Thanks for the casserole, Milly. I'll walk you to the door."

3:45 p.m.

"He's a looker," Kayla Stent says. "I can't imagine! I mean, holy baloney! Is it just wonderful?"

"What?"

She giggles. "You know..."

Emma says nothing.

Kayla blushes. Then spells the word, whispering. "The S-E-X!"

"I'm not really comfortable talking about my sex life."

"You're *not?*"

"Nope."

"*Really?*"

"Really."

"Why not?"

4:20 p.m.

"How long have you and Jack been an item?" Norma Newton says.

"Since I arrived in town, it appears."

"Well, that's the way of small towns, I suppose. Does it bother you all the single women in town and half the married ones are in love with your fiancé?"

"Are *you* in love with him?"

Norma blushes. Then says, "Have you met Darryl and Abbie Rhodes yet?"

"No."

"Wish I could be a fly on the wall when *that* happens."

"Why?"

"You'll know soon enough. I'm surprised Jack hasn't told you about Abbie. Him bein' your fiancé and all."

"We're still at that stage where we're getting to know each other better."

Norma makes a sweeping motion with her hand, indicating the living arrangements, and says, "This here goes *way* beyond gettin' to know each other."

Chapter 7

5:15 p.m.

"Thanks for allowing me in, Miss Wilson," Bill Cox says. "I hope you're finding our town a pleasant place so far."

"How can I help you, Sheriff?"

He gives her a look. "You're mighty straight-to-the-point, aren't you?"

"I doubt the County Sheriff has time to make social visits or small talk. You're obviously here for a reason."

"Mighty astute of you," he says. "You're right, by the way. I'm not normally part of the welcoming process. But your situation's a bit unique."

"How so?"

"You appear to be moving into a man's home." He pauses. "A man who's not here."

"So?"

"Well, pardon me for putting it indelicately, but we don't know a thing about you."

"We?"

"The town."

"And that's a problem because?"

"To be blunt, there's no ring on your finger. And no marriage license, from what I'm told."

"Does the state of Arkansas require an *engagement* license?"

"No, but it's customary to have an engagement ring."

"We haven't had time to shop for one yet. But I do have his house key. That should count for something."

"I'd feel better knowing he gave it to you voluntarily, and that he's not lying in a ditch somewhere."

Emma frowns. "Are you accusing me of killing Jack Russell?"

"Not yet. But from what I hear, you came into town with no suitcase, no purse, dirty clothes, and a substantial amount of cash."

"Is there a local ordinance against any of those things?"

"Not if the money's rightly yours."

"Good to know."

"Is it?"

"What?"

"The money. Is it yours?"

"How much money are *you* carrying, Sheriff?"

"That's not really your business, is it, Miss Watson?"

"It seems reasonable for you to answer the same questions you're asking me. And by the way, my name's Emma *Wilson*, not Watson."

"Can I see your ID?"

"Can I see yours?"

"I don't have to be civil here, Miss Wilson. I'm giving you the benefit of the doubt. You can't just take over a man's house without showing proof you've been invited here."

She fishes her ID from her pocket, hands it to him. He photographs it with his cell phone camera and says, "Can you confirm your date of birth?"

She does.

He returns her license. Then says, "What's your relationship with Jack Russell?"

"What's your relationship with Linda Craig?"

His face grows beet red. "I'll give you ten seconds to furnish proof of your right to be here."

"Or what?"

"Or you can spend the night in my jail."

They glare at each other a minute.

"I'm not playing around with you," he says.

"Your wife will be pleased to hear that, I expect."

She removes a folded piece of paper from her new purse and hands it over. As Cox unfolds it she says, "The letter you're reading is addressed to you, Sheriff. It's in Jack Russell's hand, authorizing me to stay in his lake house as long as I see fit. Read a little further and you'll see he admits to being my fiancé. He also authorizes me to use his personal credit card. At the end he asks you to extend me every kindness you'd show a new resident of Willow Lake, since it's his wish we eventually marry and settle down here."

Sheriff Cox studies the letter a few minutes. Then says, "You're quite the little gold digger, aren't you, Emma?"

"I'll take that as a compliment, Sheriff."

"Don't."

Chapter 8

After Sheriff Cox leaves, Emma takes her new pre-paid phone from her purse and presses a button on her speed dial for the fourth time today.

When the young man answers, Emma asks if Fanny has shown up for work yet. He says no, and asks if she'd like to leave a message. Emma says no, and asks for Fanny's cell phone number. He says he's not allowed to give out personal information. Emma sighs, and apologizes for bothering him.

She retrieves the new stepladder from the hall closet. Sets it up near the master bathroom toilet, then opens the bathroom door. Standing on the fourth step of the ladder, she pulls a permanent marker from her jeans' pocket and writes her new cell phone number on the top edge of the door. Then puts the stepladder back in the hall closet, goes to the laundry room, transfers the sheets and towels to the dryer, and sets the time.

Then she walks to the back of the house to check out the closet where Jack keeps his freezer.

9:45 p.m.

After folding her laundry and making her bed, Emma fluffs three pillows, props herself against them, opens the pack of balloons she bought at the Jessup Mall party store. It's an assortment of twenty-four balloons, all colors, shapes, sizes. She closes her eyes, sniffs the latex. Lets her fingers pick through the bag. Touches and rubs the stretchy texture. She hears herself murmur, and smiles with mild embarrassment.

She opens her eyes, selects a pink one.

Stretches it, to enhance the scent, and weaken its structure.

Puts the valve to her lips.

Chews it gently, allowing her tongue to flit around the rim, back and forth, up and down.

Breathing heavily, she works her tongue inside the valve, and feels her pulse quicken. She stops momentarily, to calm herself, then turns her attention back to the balloon, takes a deep breath, and begins blowing it up.

Balloon fetishists are generally poppers or looners, but there are endless variations of each classification. Looners love balloons, and treat them like frail children. When one pops or becomes deflated, they become devastated, as if a part of them has died.

Poppers are different.

They attach sexual emotions to balloons. A typical female popper blows a balloon till it pops, at which point she experiences an intense orgasm.

Emma's a popper, but not in the classic sense.

For her, balloons are seductive. Everything about them—the touch, smell, feel of latex against her skin—is sensual. When she blows air into a balloon she feels the life force enter it. Revels in knowing she's turned an inanimate object into a living thing.

Emma's selective. She doesn't attach feelings to random balloons. She buys packages of assorted balloons, chooses perhaps one of twenty. When she's ready, she gets completely naked, blows her select balloon to its absolute maximum, to tease herself. When she's convinced no more air can enter the balloon without bursting it, she ties off the valve, lies back on the bed, tosses it in the air, watches it fall, taps it back up with her fingers.

Looner foreplay.

Each time her fingertips make contact with the balloon, her senses become heightened. When she can stand it no longer, she spreads her legs, places the balloon snug against her triangle, squeezes her thighs gently, while touching herself. Ideally, her climax occurs at the moment the balloon pops between her thighs. When that happens, she gushes. But if the balloon proves too durable, she stabs it with a fingernail at the moment of fulfillment. This causes a different type of orgasm, less intense, less fulfilling, but like any man will tell you, there's no such thing as a bad one.

Emma's not a screamer.

A few gasps, the occasional low moan, assorted facial grimaces—and she's done.

The balloons usually burst against her inner thighs, causing a delicious sting that lasts ten or fifteen seconds. But when a balloon happens to burst against her clit, the pain is intense, long-lasting, and memorable.

Unlike most poppers, Emma doesn't require a loud explosion. In fact, she prefers a muffled pop, which is why she covers her legs with bedding after putting the balloon in place. If you were in her bedroom right now, with the lights off, you'd have no idea what's happening under the covers.

Until you hear the little gasps, and the muffled pop.

If you'll listen you'll hear...

There!

Did you hear it? And that little sound just now?

A shudder.

Moments later, she falls into a deep, sound sleep.

Doesn't even hear the sound the front door makes, as someone turns the knob and tries, unsuccessfully, to enter.

Chapter 9

10:45 a.m.

"The casserole was wonderful!" Emma says, handing Milly the empty dish.

Milly places it on the counter, opens the refrigerator, frowns.

"You hardly touched it," she says.

"I don't eat much. But what I had was truly delicious. I plan to have some more for lunch."

Milly says, "You're slim, all right. Guess that's why Jack chose you."

She glances at the kitchen countertop, then starts opening cupboards.

"Can I help you with something?" Emma says.

"Where'd you put all your canned goods?"

"They're scattered about."

Milly frowns again. "You don't have a bomb shelter, do you?"

Emma laughs. "Can I make you some coffee?"

"Might as well. I'm not planning to leave till I've told you who in town can and can't be trusted."

Emma squeezes her eyes shut, forces herself not to scream.

2:15 p.m.

The knock at the front door comes so soon after Milly's departure, Emma wonders if her new friend forgot her casserole dish. She opens the door to find Sheriff Cox standing on the front porch.

"No crimes to investigate?" she says.

"I might be investigating one right now," he says. "Mind if I come in?"

"Do I have a choice?"

"To let me in? Yes. To answer questions? No."

She motions him to enter.

"Coffee?" she says.

"I'm coffee'd out. Let's sit at the kitchen table."

They do. He says, "I'll get right to the point. Your ID doesn't check out."

"I have no idea what you're talking about."

"You're thirty years old, but the first record anyone has on you is a month's worth of wages at the Pancake House in Davis, Kentucky. And that was last month."

"I came late to the work force."

"No shit you did."

"Is it a crime not to receive a salary before attaining the age of thirty?"

"It might be, depending on how you managed to support yourself all these years without a husband or parents."

"What makes you think I have no parents?"

"Your social security number belongs to a girl whose parents died in an automobile accident twenty-one years ago."

"Did it ever cross your mind I may have inherited a substantial sum of money from their estate?"

"Not for a minute."

"Why's that?"

"According to the police report, you died in the same wreck."

"Well, here I sit, Sheriff, so whatever police report you read is obviously bogus."

"How do you explain having the same social security number as a dead girl?"

"Government ineptitude."

"Ever been married?"

"None of your business."

"Where's Jack Russell?"

"Traveling the country, seeking buyers for his business."

"Let's give him a call."

"Go ahead."

"What's his number?"

"If you'd come here last night and treated me with a modicum of respect, I would've been glad to tell you. But I don't appreciate your tone, your comments, or your demeanor."

"You've got a fancy way of talking."

"And you don't."

His lips curl into a sneer, but his voice remains civil. "I'll make you a deal, Emma. Or whatever your name is. You get Jack on the phone, let me corroborate your story, and I'll get my nose out of your business."

Emma pauses a moment, then reaches for her cell phone. She opens it, places her index finger slightly above the key pad, then closes the phone and says, "No."

"Excuse me?"

"Why should I make your job easy?"

"Why shouldn't you?"

"Because you're an asshole, Sheriff. Either arrest me, or get out of my house."

He shows her a thin smile. "It's not your house, Emma."

"I have more right to be here than you."

He stands. "For now."

"Run along, Sheriff."

4:20 p.m.

Emma puts her cell phone in her jeans' pocket, walks to the end of the hall, opens the closet door where Jack keeps his freezer. Last night she did this with the light on, but this time she closes the door and tries it in total darkness. She reaches behind the freezer, and pulls it toward her. It slides easily, twenty-four inches, same as it did last night, same as Jack said it would.

She takes a moment to think about Jack. Wonders if he's alive. If so, she hopes he shows up soon, because her story's unraveling faster than a Taylor Swift romance.

She climbs over the freezer top, turns her back to the wall, hoists herself down into the narrow hole behind the freezer, till her heels find the top step of the built-in ladder.

She descends four steps, then pulls the freezer back in place. It proves harder than she anticipated, but she's able to manage. She descends the ladder till her feet touch the concrete floor of Jack's secret room. She feels the wall for the light switch. Finds it, flips the lights on.

Funny how Milly asked about a bomb shelter this morning.

Emma takes inventory. Mini-fridge, cot, wallet, money, forty bottles of water, snacks, canned goods, can opener, paper plates, plastic utensils, wet wipes, camper's toilet, box of plastic bags for her waste, light bulbs, flashlight, batteries, ear buds, Jack's handgun, box of bullets. Extra clothing. Sheets, blanket, and pillow for the cot. Table, chair, laptop computer.

Laptop computer?

She plugs the power cable into the outlet, hits the on button, waits for it to power up. Spends the next thirty minutes typing everything she knows about Jack into three different search engines, but nothing comes up.

That's a good thing. If his plane crashed, it would have been reported by now. But the fact he's not here could mean someone killed him and dumped his body in a swamp.

She turns off the computer, walks to the ladder, climbs the first step...

...And hears someone kick the back door open!

She starts to flip the light off, then decides it's safer to keep it on. At least she won't trip over something and make a noise.

She crosses the floor, sits on the cot, loads the gun. Listens to the heavy footsteps moving slowly down the hall above her. Hears a man's voice calling to her in a mocking way.

"Are you hiding, Emma? I know you're in here. Come out, come out, wherever you are! Emma?"

She knows exactly where he is by his footsteps and running commentary.

"Are you in the laundry room? No? How about the coat closet? No? Maybe you're in the powder room? No? Could you possibly be hiding behind...the *couch*? No? Where *are* you, Emma?"

Even though his voice is high and creepy, she can tell he's a big man. He's almost certainly drunk, as well.

"Are you upstairs, Emma?"

She hears him climb the steps.

"What's up here, Emma? A bedroom? Another bathroom? Maybe I'll give you a bath. Would you like that, Emma?"

He continues speaking in a weird, sing-song voice, but he's too far away for her to make out the exact words.

Until he comes back down the stairs.

She hears him walking directly above her, hears him open the door to the closet above her, where the freezer is kept.

"Don't tell me you're hiding in the freezer!"

She doesn't hear him turn the closet light on, or open the freezer, but she assumes he does. She lifts the gun, aims it at the top of the built-in ladder. She can literally see the bottom of the freezer. If he happens to pull it toward him and lean over it, he'll see the open area that leads to the secret room. If Jack's gun works, she'll blow him away as he descends the ladder.

He'll have no chance of surviving if he descends the ladder.

If Jack's gun works.

If she has the guts to pull the trigger.

She doesn't hear him close the freezer, or turn off the light, but she does hear him close the closet door.

"I saved the master bedroom for last," he says.

Emma gives a sigh of relief when she hears him say, "Are you under the bed? No? How about the bedroom closets? No? The bathroom? Are you hiding in the shower, Emma? I hope you're naked! I surely do hope you're naked!"

A moment goes by quietly, then she hears him say, "My, my! What do we have here?"

Then he goes quiet.

She knows he's up there, in the master bedroom, but doing what?

Hiding?

Waiting for her to return?

Time passes.

No problem, she can wait him out. Thank God she was in the secret room when he showed up. She can sit tight for weeks, if need be.

Emma waits patiently for another twenty minutes, then hears a pop. The type of pop that can only come from...

Her balloons! The bastard has her balloons!

A moment passes, then...

Pop!

Emma makes a face, squeezes her eyes shut, tries to force her mind not to think about the scent of latex, the texture, the...

Pop!

Her face flushes hot. She swallows. Feels her nipples grow hard as she imagines the life force filling a balloon. But what shape? What size? What color? Not knowing which ones he selected is making her crazy.

Pop!

Oh!

She's...

Pop!

Oh, my God!

She's...*Omigod!* Did she just have an accident?

She did.

But...did she scream?

No. At least, she doesn't think so.

But if he pops another one she will. Because that will take her to Multiple Land, a place she's never been.

She listens carefully.

Is he blowing up another one?

If he is, she's toast.

She prays he s not.

But secretly hopes he is.

She closes her eyes. Feels her hand moving toward...

No! She can't let it happen. If she cries out, she'll have to kill him.

Whoever he is.

Thankfully, she hears him walking again. Hears him leave the master bedroom. Hears him walk down the hallway toward the back door. Hears his creepy voice say, "I'll be back!"

Will he?

She hears the door slam shut.

Has he, in fact, gone?

She carefully places Jack's gun on the floor, then lies down on the cot.

Two hours later she turns off the secret room light, climbs up the ladder, pushes the freezer away from the wall, climbs over it, puts it back in place, and checks the condition of the back door. She closes it, notices the frame's intact. She gets a hammer and three quarters, presses the quarters between the door and the jamb, and pounds them flush against the frame. It's not perfect, but it'll do, since she'll be spending her nights in Jack's secret room for the time being.

She goes to the master bedroom, sees five burst balloons on her bed, one of her bras, and a pair of her panties.

She starts shaking, realizing what he did prior to bursting the balloons.

She goes to the kitchen, removes a knife from the drawer, brings it back to the bedroom, uses it to lift her soiled bra and panties from the bed.

She retches once, twice, in horror and disgust, and nearly drops them on the floor, but manages to carry them down the hall, holding them as far away from her as possible, while trying not to gag. She makes her way to the kitchen, drops her bra, panties, and knife in the trash.

On the way back to the bedroom, she grabs a tissue, uses it to collect the balloon pieces, tosses them in the master bathroom trash basket.

Then she changes into running clothes.

Chapter 10

Emma turns the porch light on, goes outside, strains her eyes to see if the kid in the Ford pickup is spying on her again. If he is, she can't tell. Too much tree cover. But really, what difference would it make? She can't very well grab his ear and threaten him like her cabbie, Frank Sturgiss, did. She stretches a few minutes, walks down the porch steps, notices a tiny red dot glowing in the grass a few feet away. Walks over, reaches down to see what it is, but it's disappeared. She gives up the search, starts jogging Leeds Road in the same direction Frank the cabbie walked yesterday morning. Frank's been gone about thirty hours, and though she barely knew the man, she misses him. Felt a lot safer when he was around.

Leeds Road runs north of Willow Lake. If you enter from the south, Jack Russell's place is second on the left. During tourist season, all these homes will be filled to the rafters with families. But tonight, the first four houses she passes are empty.

Jack's neighborhood is on a peninsula of land that surrounds a large, wooded hill, where Frank says the townies hang out. Normally Emma wouldn't run in a strange place this close to dusk, but she's had a rough three days, needs to unwind, and wants to know where her neighbors are.

Leeds Road circles the hill for three-fourths of a mile. In that stretch, Emma sees evidence of four permanent residents. The closest is only three hundred yards away, which is reassuring. Maybe she'll pay them a visit tomorrow.

When Leeds dead-ends at Route 53, Emma turns left, runs a quarter mile to Thread Hill, which offers another mile of lakefront houses. When the road ends at the woods, she turns around, heads back the way she came. Emma can comfortably run an eight-minute pace for an hour, but it's getting darker now, so she decides to cut her run short. When she gets back to Jack's house, she finds a midnight-blue Mustang parked in the driveway.

Approaching from the rear, she sees the windows are fogged. Should she circle around to the back of the house? Or tap on the trunk to see who gets out of the car?

She opts to tap on the trunk, figuring to keep the car between her and the bad guy, should there be a bad guy. Just as she's about to tap, she thinks, *what if there are two men in the car?*

By then it doesn't matter.

The driver's door opens, a man climbs out. A very large, very angry man who says, "Emma Wilson?"

She recognizes the voice. Heard it three hours ago, in her home, before he masturbated on her underwear. What a charmer.

But he's not being charming now.

The term "seething with anger" comes to mind. As does drunk. And redneck. And...did she mention angry?

"Emma *Wilson*?" he repeats, through clenched teeth.

"Yes?"

"I'm Darryl Rhodes. Invite me in."

"Last time you were here you left some DNA in my bra and panties."

"I won't ask you again."

"Good. Because you'd get the same response. No! Now fuck off, Darryl."

Darryl doesn't like her response. Likes it so little, he looks ready to lunge at her. Emma tenses, ready to sprint. Suddenly the passenger door opens, and a young lady who can't be more than twenty gets out. As she does, the interior light allows Emma to see extensive cuts and bruises on her face.

"You must be Abbie," she says.

"Yes ma'am."

"Why are you here?"

Darryl looks across the car at his young wife, curls his lips into a sneer as ugly as a puss wound. "Tell her, bitch."

Abbie gives him a pleading look, then gives up and says, "I had sex with your fiancé."

Darryl says, "Tell her *when.*"

"Last month."

Chapter 11

"You hear that?" Darryl says. "Your fiancé was cheatin' on you last month with this *whore*! What do you think about *that*?"

Emma says, "I don't approve of your tone, nor do I tolerate drunks on my property."

"Is that right? Well, it ain't your property, though, is it?"

"Not yet. Which is all the more reason not to let you stay. You've delivered your message. Jack cheated on me. Anything else?"

"Yeah, I got somethin' else. Are them tits of yours real?"

"I can't think of a single reason to answer that question."

"I got one. Your fiancé fucked my *wife*!"

Emma pauses a minute, then says, "If you've got more to say about that, you'll have to sit on the porch to do it. Otherwise, leave."

"Where will Abbie sit?"

"Wherever she likes."

He gives Abbie a look. "Guess you'll be sittin' beside me on the porch, Sugar Plum."

She reluctantly walks toward him, follows him up the steps, takes a seat beside him.

Emma knows beyond a doubt she can outrun this giant hillbilly at any distance. The fact he's twenty feet away, drunk, and sitting down, makes her safe as Fort Knox. Nevertheless, she reminds herself to remain alert in case things turn ugly.

"You didn't answer me, Emma," Darryl says. "How does it make you feel that the man you exchanged solemn promises with was fuckin' a married woman no more'n a month ago?"

Emma says, "Is that true, Abbie?"

"Yes, ma'am. I'm real sorry."

"I believe you. Do you plan to do it again?"

She looks at her husband, then back at Emma. "No ma'am."

"You promise?"

"Yes, ma'am."

"Good. I forgive you."

"You do?" Abbie says.

"Yes, of course."

Darryl says, "*What? You what?*"

"She's young. She made a mistake. I forgive her."

"You don't *give* a shit?"

"Not much reason to be upset at this point. Whatever brought them together was obviously beyond my control. If it's not going to happen again, Abbie and I can still be friends."

"*Friends?*" Darryl yells. "You want to be *friends?*"

Abbie gives her a hopeful look.

Emma says, "I mean that, Abbie. But I'll hold you to your promise about Jack."

Abbie nods.

Emma notices a tiny red dot dancing on the wooden column by the porch steps. Some sort of miniature Arkansas firefly. Then, just as suddenly as before, it's gone.

"Well, if this don't just beat the fuckin' band!" Darryl says. "What the hell kind of liberal bullshit *is* this? Do you know what him and her *did?*"

"No. And I don't care. It's in the past."

"She *fornicated* with your *fiancé*. She had oral sex. That means she put her mouth—"

"I'm quite aware what it means. I also know what it's like to be beaten by a man who gets all his confidence from a bottle. Whatever she did, it's clear she's paid for it a hundred times over by having to deal with you."

"He pulled her *panties* down. He saw...*everything*! Every damn thing she's got. He *touched* her. Kissed her *privates*! And was that enough for him? Hell *no*! He bent her over and—"

Emma holds up her hand. "That's enough, Darryl."

"*Your fiancé fucked my wife!*"

"Let me see if I've got this straight. My fiancé, Jack Russell, fucked your wife. Saw her private parts. Touched them. They had oral sex."

"And anal!"

Emma looks at Abbie. "You did?"

Abbie hangs her head. "Yes, ma'am."

Emma says, "Ouch."

"That all you got to say?" Darryl yells.

"It's what comes to mind."

"Well, I'll tell you what comes to *my* mind. I got a free pass comin'. You know what that means?"

"You want to fuck Jack Russell, too?"

"*What? Hell* no!"

"Then I shudder to think what's rattling around in your head."

"You'll be shudderin', all right. It means fair is fair. I get a free pass to ride the ride. Your man soiled my woman, and turn about's fair play. I'm gonna have my way with you, Emma, and Abbie's gonna watch. She's gonna sit there and watch every damn thing we do."

Emma says, "Abbie, you're forgiven. Please feel free to visit me any time. You can spend the night tonight if you like. In fact, I recommend it." She turns her gaze to Darryl and says, "I hope I don't have to explain that legal sex requires consent, even in Arkansas. Anything outside that is rape."

"I got a free pass. I'm gonna ride my ride."

"Your free pass doesn't work at this carnival, Darryl. Go home and sleep it off."

"You think you can talk to me like that?"

"I must be crazy, right?"

As Darryl tenses, Emma glances behind her to make sure there's nothing to trip over if she needs to turn and sprint. She hears a click, turns back to see Darryl holding a gun on her.

Shit!

She didn't see that coming.

What are the chances he could shoot and miss?

On the one hand, he's pretty wasted. On the other, he's got the porch light behind him, which makes her a highly visible target. He's also a redneck, and in Emma's experience, most rednecks are pretty adept at drunken night-shooting.

Darryl staggers down the steps. They're twelve feet apart. Emma's moment of opportunity—if there *was* one—has passed.

She's a sitting duck.

"Take off your clothes," he says. "Every stitch. Then we'll go inside and party."

"Fuck you, Darryl," Emma says.

She takes a step back.

He closes the distance to eight feet. Props his left hand under the butt of his handgun and eases into a shooter's stance.

"I *will* fucking blow you away," he says. "And kill Abbie right where she sits. You know why? 'Cause I don't really give a shit. I got nothin' to live for. Jack Russell seen to that. Now peel them clothes off or I'll pistol whip the shit out of you and rip 'em off myself."

Emma pauses a moment, then lifts her jog bra, exposing herself. As it clears her shoulders, it momentarily blocks her vision. She can't see Darryl's reaction, but hears him make a strange sound, like all the wind suddenly escaped his body. By the time her jog bra's above her head, Darryl's on the ground.

"*Omigod!*" Abbie screams.

Emma rushes toward him, delivers a hard kick to his face. And instantly realizes the reaction his body makes is all wrong.

She kneels beside him, checks his pulse.

"Holy shit!" she says. "I think he's dead!"

Abbie screams and runs down the road. Emma considers chasing after her, but decides the neighbors will find Abbie soon enough.

Chapter 12

Sheriff Cox frowns, puts his TV on mute, sets his bourbon on the coffee table, checks his caller ID, and sighs.

"What's up, Nelda?" he says. "Bobcats again?"

"No, Sheriff. This time I'm callin' about Abbie Rhodes."

"What about her?"

"She was runnin' down the road just now, screamin' bloody murder."

"In *your* neighborhood?"

"Yup."

"Darryl been drinking again?"

"Can't say for sure. She ain't makin' a whole lot of sense right now."

"What's she saying, exactly?"

"Somethin' about the new lady killin' Darryl."

"*What?*"

"You know the new lady in town? The one stayin' at Jack Russell's place? We ain't met her yet, though we saw her joggin' the road a few minutes ago."

"Emma Wilson?"

"I reckon that's her name. Anyway, Abbie says she done killed Darryl just now."

"He probably passed out drunk in Jack's yard. But just to be on the safe side, stay put till I get there, okay?"

"No problem. You probably already know how much I hate corpses. 'Specially after buryin' Jimmy last week."

"Jimmy?"

"Our possum."

"I'm on my way. Are you home?"

"Yup."

"Abbie with you?"

"Uh huh."

"And Emma Wilson?"

"She's at Jack Russell's, far as I know. With Darryl's body, if Abbie's to be believed. 'Course, she's been known to take drugs. I sent Harlan over to check it out."

"I wish you hadn't done that. It could be dangerous."

"Harlan'll be fine. He took his turkey gun."

You just knew he would, Sheriff Cox thinks. He switches the call to speaker, rushes to his car, climbs in, fires the engine.

"I'll check Jack's place first, then get to you soon as I can. Meanwhile, do me a favor and put Abbie on the phone."

He covers a mile while waiting for Abbie to pick up. When she finally does, she yells, "Emma Wilson kilt him, Sheriff!"

"She killed Darryl? You're certain?"

"I ought to be! I was right there, sittin' on the porch when it happened!"

"You saw Emma kill Darryl?"

"Yes, sir."

"You witnessed the murder."

"Yes, sir."

"And you're certain he's dead?"

"Yes, sir. Emma took his pulse and declared him dead on the spot."

"Darryl's a big man."

"Yes, sir."

"Was he drinking?"

"Darryl's *always* drinkin'."

"Could he have passed out, maybe suffered a heart attack?"

"Nope. This is somethin' she done to him, all by herself."

"Did she shoot him?"

"No, sir."

"*Stab* him?"

"No, sir."

Sheriff Cox reminds himself that talking to Abbie Rhodes is like talking to a slow-witted eight-year old.

"Abbie, try to concentrate," he says, making an effort to keep the frustration out of his voice. "You're claiming that Emma Wilson, who stands five-six, weighs a hundred-twenty pounds, killed your husband, Darryl, who's six-six, and weighs three hundred pounds."

"Yes, sir."

"Well, if she didn't shoot or stab Darryl, how the hell did she manage to *kill* him?"

"She flashed her tits at him."

Chapter 13

Emma Wilson's far and away the prettiest woman Sheriff Cox has ever seen in person, and he'll freely admit that interviewing her without glancing below her neck was tough duty. But he seriously doubts the woman's tits are lethal. Nor does he intend to include Abbie's claim in the police report. Doing so would make him the laughing stock of the Little Rock Law Enforcement Convention next month.

He tries it out in his head: "Sheriff Cox, did you conduct a thorough search before uncovering the murder weapons?"

I can honestly say I did my breast work on this case.

"Were the nipples actively involved?"

I left tit to the boobs at the coroner's office to make that determination.

"How did you secure the crime scene?"

With a giant bra.

"Did you personally handle the murder weapons?"

Not to my complete satisfaction.

Chapter 14

Emma raises her flashlight from Darryl's body, trains the beam toward the sound she hears in the road. Sees a man with a shotgun, moving toward her at a fast clip.

She jumps to her feet, runs to the porch, but stops when he yells, "Ma'am, I'm Harlan Doody, your neighbor. Are you all right?"

"This man's been shot," Emma says.

"By you?"

"No, of course not!"

By the time these words have passed between them, Harlan's standing over Darryl's body. He says, "Can you come down here and shine your flashlight on him?"

Emma can see Harlan's an old man. Then again, he's holding a shotgun.

She says, "Will you put your gun down?"

Harlan can see Emma's not armed. Then again, *someone* shot Darryl.

He says, "Anyone else here with you?"

"No."

"Then who shot this ugly bastard?"

"I have no idea, but I'm glad they did. He tried to rape me."

"That sounds like Darryl, all right," Harlan says.

He places his shotgun on the grass. Emma walks down, shines the light on Darryl's corpse.

"Looks like a high-powered rifle shot to the forehead," Harlan says. "He was dead 'fore he hit the ground."

"The shot came from up there," she says, pointing behind Harlan. "On the hill."

Harlan turns to look. "That'd be a helluva shot. You sure it came from up there?"

"It had to." She points her flashlight about ten feet behind them, toward the road. "I was standing there, Abbie was sitting on the porch. If someone was holding a rifle on Darryl from the road, I would have heard him, and Darryl and Abbie would have seen him."

"Well, this don't appear to be the work of a local rifle."

"No one here has a high-powered rifle?"

"Not with a silencer."

"Silencer?"

"Did you hear the shot?"

She pauses a second. "No."

"Neither did Abbie. Not to mention Nelda and me were on the porch when all this happened. If a shot was fired, we'd of heard it. Unless..—"

"Unless the shooter used a silencer."

He points to the road and says, "We can tell that much to Sheriff Cox, I reckon."

Emma looks up, sees the flashing lights of Sheriff Cox's cruiser turning onto Leeds Road from the highway.

Chapter 15

Assuming there are no suspects to apprehend, or victims needing medical assistance, the police procedures manual says the first arriving officer at a possible homicide should call for backup, protect the crime scene, and document all observations. Specific personnel should be contacted as soon as possible, including immediate supervisor, crime scene investigator, evidence technicians, homicide detective, coroner, and enough patrolmen to properly secure and manage the crime scene, interview witnesses, and canvass the area.

Since Sheriff Cox has but three deputies, two of which are on vacation, he's clearly in over his head. He calls those he can reach, and presses Emma, Harlan, and the rest of the neighbors into service, including Abbie Rhodes, who keeps insisting Emma's breasts are responsible for her husband's death. Even after being told Darryl was shot with a high-powered rifle.

"Aren't you gonna arrest her, Sheriff?" Abbie asks.

"Did you see Emma Wilson holding a high-powered rifle?" Sheriff Cox asks. "Or any rifle at all?"

"No. But that don't change the fact that one minute she's standin' there showin' her boobs, and the next minute Darryl's dead."

"I can't have this discussion right now."

"*Don't look at her tits!*" Abbie shouts to anyone who'll listen.

More than an hour passes before the proper personnel show up from neighboring cities and towns, and by then half the citizens of Willow Lake have descended on the crime scene, each with a theory and suspect firmly in mind.

But the only theory that sounds credible to Sheriff Cox is the one proposed by Ellwood Fillmore.

Sheriff Cox takes notes while questioning him. "You're saying Emma's cab driver threatened your parents at the grocery store yesterday morning? Then grabbed you by the ear and threatened you with bodily harm?"

"Yes, sir."

"You remember his exact words?" Sheriff Cox says.

"He said, 'Normally I'd go ahead and kill you.' Then he said, 'As long as I'm in a position to keep Emma safe, I will.'"

Sheriff Cox finds Emma and says, "Tell me about your cab driver. And don't leave anything out, or I'll arrest you for obstruction of justice."

He removes the pen and notebook from his pocket and says, "Start with his name."

"Frank Sturgiss."

"And where's he from?"

"Memphis."

"We're a long way from Memphis."

"Do you expect me to confirm that?"

He sighs. "Nothing's easy with you, is it, Emma?"

"No. And don't forget it, Sheriff."

He takes a deep breath, then says, "How long have you known Mr. Sturgiss?"

"I met him two nights ago at the Memphis airport. He was the next cab in line."

"I don't believe you."

"Darn."

"Why would a cab driver you barely know feel protective enough to threaten Ellwood Fillmore for parking near your house?"

"Here's an idea. Why don't you ask *him?*"

"You got his phone number?"

"I do."

Emma goes in the house, comes back with Frank's business card, hands it to Sheriff Cox.

"I'll need Jack's phone number, too."

"Who?"

"Jack Russell. Your fiancé?"

"Why?"

"A murder has been committed on his property."

"Right. Hang on a minute."

She turns, starts heading back to the house.

"Wait!" Sheriff Cox says. "Where are you going?"

"To get Jack's cell phone number."

"You're telling me you don't know your own fiancé's cell phone number by heart?"

"Not off-hand. I usually just press a number on speed dial."

"Uh huh. So what's *your* cell phone number?"

"I'll get my phone and tell you."

"You don't know your *own* number?"

"It's a new one. I got it at the mall this morning."

"What was your old number?"

"This is the first cell phone I've ever owned."

"I thought you said Jack's number was programmed in your cell phone."

"I was referring to my girlfriend's cell phone. She let me use it from time to time."

"What's your girlfriend's name?"

"None of your business."

"What were you doing in Memphis, Tennessee, two nights ago?"

"Hailing a cab."

"Besides that."

"None of your business."

"Get me Jack's number. Now!"

Emma leaves to get Jack's number, and never comes back.

Chapter 16

Between the sudden arrival of the evidence-gathering team at the crime scene, the field report from those who searched the hill, crowd-control issues, interviews with possible witnesses, and the arrival of the coroner—it takes Sheriff Cox fifteen minutes to realize Emma hasn't returned. He and some volunteers search the house and back yard, then he tells them to move the search to the front yard and road, where a hundred townies have gathered. Then he calls in an APB on a cab with Tennessee plates. He knows Emma didn't kill Darryl, but finds it likely the cab driver did. If so, he either kidnapped her, or she's run off with him.

At least that's the working theory.

The evidence team is already in the kitchen, which means Sheriff Cox will need to rope off the house so they can do their job without interruption. He doubts they'll get much, but the fingerprints and DNA samples might help him determine Emma's identity, if she's ever been arrested. If so, who knows *what* they might be able to uncover?

His thoughts are interrupted by the crackling sound from his walkie-talkie. He presses the button and says, "Sheriff Cox."

"Sheriff? You'll want to see this before we tag it and send it off to the lab," Ghostly Edwards says.

"Where are you, Ghostly?"

"Kitchen."

Sheriff Cox enters, sees Ghostly holding a plastic trash bag.

"What have you found?"

"Bra, knife, pair of panties."

"Emma Wilson's bra and panties?"

"Size appears right."

"And the knife?"

"If I counted correctly, there's one missing from the drawer."

He opens the bag.

Sheriff Cox looks inside and says, "That's a regular knife. Tableware."

"It is," Ghostly says. "But who'd throw away a perfectly fine piece of tableware?"

Sheriff adds, "Not to mention a bra and panties."

"I can answer that part. They're soiled."

"Soiled? How?"

"My guess? Semen stains. In copious quantities."

"What's that supposed to mean?"

"Are you familiar with the term backflow?"

"Pretend I'm not."

"When a man ejaculates into a woman's vagina, less than twenty percent of the sperm swims in the right direction." He winks, then adds, "Which explains why either you or Mrs. Cox has to sleep on the wet spot every night."

Sheriff Cox frowns. "How about you give me more point and less commentary?"

Ghostly says, "Ejaculate enters the vagina in a thick, milky consistency. After a few minutes, it liquefies, and starts seeping back out."

"Meaning?"

"If a woman puts her panties back on after sex, some of the sperm will collect in them. We call it backflow."

"You think that's what happened here?"

"No."

"Excuse me?"

"No, that's not what happened here."

"It's not?"

"Of *course* not!"

Sheriff frowns again and yells, "Then why the hell did you *tell* me all that?"

"Because backflow typically leaves residual stains, not pools."

"So?"

"This is too much sperm. *Way* too much!"

"What if it was a big load?"

"That might explain the panties. But the bra?"

"What about it?"

"One of the cups is wet. And has been for more than an hour."

"You can tell how old the stains are?"

"No. But people have been coming in and out of here for hours, right? I doubt Emma had the time or opportunity to engage in coitus."

Sheriff Cox removes his hat, runs a hand through his hair, sighs, puts his hat back on and says, "You got a theory?"

Ghostly smiles. "I do."

"Let's hear it."

"I believe someone, probably Darryl Rhodes, jacked off on her bra, then used her panties to wipe himself dry."

"Charming."

"It's just a theory."

"Why didn't Emma just wash her underwear?"

"I'm betting she wasn't here when it happened. Probably saw what he'd done to her clothes and was disgusted. Probably came home from jogging, like she said, found Darryl in the house. He came out, Emma—or someone else—shot him."

"What about Abbie?"

"Maybe she was in the house with him."

"And the knife?"

"My guess is she went into the house after Abbie ran down the street. She went to the bedroom to gather her things to make a run for it, saw the underwear on the floor, used a knife to carry her bra and panties so she wouldn't have to touch them."

"Then put them in the trash bag?"

"That's my guess."

Sheriff Cox says, "Unless the knife was already in the bedroom, which I doubt, she'd have to make a trip to the kitchen to get it. Then back to the bedroom. Then back to the kitchen to toss it out. Then back to the bedroom to gather her things."

"So?"

"You think she'd take the time to do all that with Abbie running down the road, screaming? Wouldn't she just leave the bra and panties where she found them?"

"She's a woman."

"So?"

"Some women don't want to leave a mess behind. Even if it means getting caught."

Sheriff Cox frowns for the third time since beginning the discussion with Ghostly. "You know what I think?"

"What's that?"

"I think you're right about Darryl, and the bra and panties. Except I think Darryl came here to discuss the rumor about Jack and Abbie. He probably told Abbie to stay in the car while he talked to Emma. But Emma was out jogging, so she didn't answer the door. We've got proof someone kicked the back door open, and I expect it was Darryl. He probably searched the house for valuables, found her underwear drawer, and got sidetracked. I expect Abbie got tired of waiting, came in through the back door, saw what her husband had just done. I expect she got the knife from the kitchen, used it to carry the bra and panties to the trash bag. Then they both went out the back door and ran into Emma, who'd just finished her jog."

"Those TV cop shows have nothing on us," Ghostly says. Except that on TV, DNA samples come back from the lab before the end of the show. Here it takes three months."

"Any way you can rush it? This is a murder investigation, after all."

"Rushing it means three months. But it *has* to be Darryl's sperm. If not, whose could it possibly be?"

"Actually, I can think of two people. One, Frank Sturgiss, the cab driver."

"And the other?"

"Jack Russell."

Chapter 17

Down below, in the secret room, Emma listens and waits. She hears endless footsteps walking up and down the hallway, hears pieces of conversations. The last thing she hears before everything goes quiet is Sheriff Cox instructing his deputy to park on the hill and keep an eye out in case Emma, Frank Sturgis, or Jack Russell shows up. She waits a few minutes longer, then focuses her attention on the last thing Jack told her about the secret room...

Part Two:
HOW THEY MET

Chapter 1

Five Days Earlier.
Davis, Kentucky, Friday Night.
Jack Tallow, a.k.a. Jack Russell
Jill Whittaker, a.k.a. Emma Wilson

The entertainment reporter called Favors Strip Club an institution.

So's Eddyville State Prison, Jack thinks, entering the worst club he's ever seen. *This place isn't a dump*, he decides. *It's a shithole, gone to seed.*

The reporter wrote, "The bar, a full-service oasis, caters to the hottest women you'll find in any club."

Jack agrees the women are hot. So are the men. But only because the air conditioning system is woefully inadequate.

He grabs one of several empty seats at the bar.

Bartender says, "What'll you have?"

She's...female, Jack decides, though he wouldn't put money on it. He orders a scotch, nods at the woman who quickly grabs one of the two empty seats beside him. The cute brunette in shorts and tank top who's definitely female.

She says, "You read the write up."

"I did."

"And?"

"The reporter should be arrested for fraud," Jack says.

"I know, right?" she says. "He's working off a debt."

"He must've owed a lot."

She smiles. "Still, it worked."

"How so?"

"It got *you* here."

"Once."

"Once might be enough."

"That sounds promising."

She says, "I'm glad you found us. Even though it's not your type of place."

He looks around. "What sort of place do you see me in?"

"Air conditioned. Elegant. High class call girls."

"Call girls?"

"I'd think so."

He studies her body a moment. "You're a dancer?"

She nods. "I'm the new girl. Lace."

"Lace?"

She nods.

"You're not a lap dancer."

"I'm not?"

"I mean, you seem...ah—"

She waits him out, daring him to say it. Finally, he does. "You seem a little old for lap dancing. No offense."

"I'm thirty."

"I hope you didn't take that wrong. I think you're extremely attractive."

"That's actually more offensive than calling me 'a little old.'"

"I don't understand."

"Of course you don't. But like you say, older women are attractive."

"And that's insulting because?"

"Younger women are cute. Adorable. Gorgeous. You're calling me a pocket book instead of a hand bag."

"I believe I said extremely attractive. I didn't say that to upset you."

"I'm not upset. I'm just being honest about my age. And you're right."

"About what?"

"I'm not a lap dancer. I'm a stage stripper."

Jack looks her over again and says, "Doesn't fit."

"What doesn't?"

"You. In this place. Stripping."

"What should I be doing?"

"Raising your kids. With a wealthy husband. In the suburbs."

"A trophy wife?"

"Yes. And that's a compliment."

"So we're both out of our element," she says.

"You're sure about that?"

She laughs. "I'm not sure about anything, mister. That's why I'm here instead of where I ought to be. The question is why are you reading reviews about a place like this?"

"Never hurts to meet new people."

She extends her hand. "In that case, what's your name?"

He takes her hand, shakes it. "Leather."

"Leather?"

He nods.

"That's a bullshit name," she says.

"So's Lace."

"It's my stage name."

"Then I guess we're Leather and Lace," he says.

"I don't like it."

"You won't like my real name much, either."

"Try me."

"You first."

"I'm Jill. Jill Whittaker."

"Jack Tallow."

"Tallow?"

"Uh huh."

"Tallow, like the stuff in soap and candles?"

"Tallow's actually rendered beef or mutton fat. But yeah, they make soap and candles from it. Or used to, anyway."

She laughs.

He says, "I can go back to Leather if you like."

"No. I like Jack Tallow."

They look at each other a minute. Jill says, "We should do it!"

"We should?"

"Wouldn't it be funny if we did?"

"*Funny?* That's not the word I'd choose."

"Where's ycur sense of humor?"

"I'm sorry. What are we talking about?"

"Going up the hill, of course."

"Excuse me?"

"The nursery rhyme? Jack and Jill went up the hill to fetch a pail of water?"

He shakes his head and says, "For a minute I thought you were offering me sex."

She locks her eyes on his and says, "If I were, how much would you pay?"

Chapter 2

"I wouldn't pay for sex," Jack says.

"Ever?"

"No. But I'm generous."

"What's that mean?"

"It means if I had a girlfriend who needed a thousand bucks for a new refrigerator, or tires for her car, all she'd have to do is ask."

"Sounds like the same thing to me," she says.

"Which proves you're not a district attorney."

"Good point. Can I ask you something?"

"Go ahead."

"Could a thirty-year-old mother of two be your girlfriend?"

"If she looked like you, she could."

Jill smiles. "And if someone who looks like me happened to be interested, how would she let you know without appearing to be a slut?"

"She'd say yes to a real date."

"You mean like dinner and dancing? That kind of date?"

"That's exactly what I mean."

"Well, you've surprised me. This is a first."

"Does that mean you're interested?"

"I don't get off work till two. That's pretty late for dinner and dancing."

"We could wait till your day off."

"Three problems with that idea," she says.

"Tell me."

"First, the club prohibits us from dating customers, and I need this job. Second, I spend my days off with my kids."

"And third?"

"My car needs tires right *now*."

"Three solutions," Jack says. "First, I'm not a customer."

"You ordered a drink."

"I haven't got it yet. When it comes, I'll send it back. Second, you'll hire a babysitter. My treat. And third—"

He reaches into his suit jacket, removes a bank envelope, and places it on her lap.

"For me?" she says.

"You'll need tires to drive to the restaurant. When's your day off?"

"Sunday and Monday. But Sunday's reserved for my girls."

"Monday then," Jack says.

"You're trusting me to show up?"

"Yes, absolutely."

"What if I don't?"

"I'll have to find a new girlfriend."

Chapter 3

Jill thinks it over a minute. "You haven't asked for my address."

"You've got daughters. You can't give your address to a guy you barely know."

"Good point. Which restaurant did you have in mind?"

"Le Pirouette."

An angry look darkens her face. "What the fuck's going on here?"

"A dinner invitation. But you seem upset, somehow."

"Look," she says, "we both know what this is. If you want to dress it up and call it a real date, I'm fine with that. But don't give me a thousand bucks and ask me to meet you at a swanky restaurant like Le Pirouette."

"Why not?"

"Because I'd have to spend half the contents of this envelope on a dress to wear. And I can't tell you how badly I need every nickel. And more."

Jack removes another envelope from his pocket, places it on her lap. "Perhaps this will help you buy a suitable dress."

Jill takes a deep breath, holds it, then sighs. "I don't wish to appear ungrateful..."

"But?"

"A five hundred dollar dress is an extravagance. An indulgence. A waste of resources."

"Not to me."

"Why, because you're rich?"

"Because I'd love to see it on you."

"And perhaps off me, after our date?"

"I'd be lying if I said no. But that will be entirely up to you."

"Can I keep whatever's left over after buying the dress?"

"Of course. This is a gift, not a payment. No strings attached."

She eyes him carefully. "Why are you doing this?"

"Doing what?"

"For lack of a better word? Slumming. Does it make you feel powerful to toss this type of money around? I'm supposed to what, swoon over you? Could you possibly be more pompous or arrogant?"

"I thought it'd be fun for you. Thought you'd enjoy buying a nice dress, getting your hair and nails done, going somewhere special for dinner."

"You make me sound like Little Orphan Annie. Like I'm some country bumkin who'd be lucky to get a date to the flippin' Pancake House."

Jack notices the cocktail straws stacked in a glass tumbler on the counter. He grabs one, bends it in half, straightens it, then gives it a final look before saying, "Are you always this difficult to date?"

"My dates are pretty straight-forward, as you might expect, based on the way I came onto you earlier."

She looks around the room a moment, then turns her focus back to Jack. "I'll admit it's a generous offer," she says. "And you're showing a lot of respect."

"But?"

"But there's something in your attitude that annoys the shit out of me."

"What is that, do you suppose?"

"I don't like being talked down to, Jack. You're no better than me."

"I agree."

"Just because you've got money, doesn't make you better."

"Who said it does?"

"Your condescending attitude says it. Why are you doing this? You want a fuck? I'll *sell* you a fuck. For *half* what you've tossed in my lap."

"Is that all you want? A fuck?"

"That's what's honest. And it would prevent me having to get all dressed up and tell my kids their mom's going out on a big date at a fancy restaurant with a rich, handsome man."

"You think I'm handsome?"

"Oh, fuck *you!*"

"Excuse me?"

"Like it's a big surprise. Like you haven't heard it every single day of your pampered life."

"Pampered?"

"I don't want my daughters wasting a second's worth of hope on a dream that'll never come true."

"What dream? I don't understand."

"Of *course* you don't! That's the problem when you dress the truth up in fancy clothes."

Jack stares at her blankly.

Jill says, "You'll meet me for dinner and dancing. You'll see me all dressed up and say all the right things. All evening you'll search my eyes to see if you've put hope in them. That's what gets you off, I think. You'll give me this dream date, make me princess for a day, bang the shit out of me, then move along and find the next urchin."

"Urchin?"

"You come in here and drop two thousand bucks in my lap? Tell me to buy myself a dress for the big occasion? Well, fuck *you*!"

Jack says nothing, content to listen with utter fascination.

Jill says, "You're an asshole. A complete and utter asshole."

Though she's indignant, her eyes smoldering with anger, Jack notices she hasn't returned the envelopes.

He says, "What's the real issue here?"

Chapter 4

It takes a minute, but eventually Jill's features soften a bit. "The envelopes you gave me were pre-packaged. If I hadn't shown up you'd have given the same spiel and money to whoever happened along."

"You'd feel more special if I sat here in front of all these people and counted out two thousand dollars and handed it to you? Does that make sense from a safety standpoint?"

She says, "Smoothness aside, you walked in here with the intention of making some girl your princess for a day."

"It seems you've made up your mind about that, so there's not much point in arguing."

"That's a fancy way of admitting I'm right."

"But you're not."

"Prove it."

Jack sighs. "You're upset because I came here with a plan to find a woman and pay her to go on a romantic date with me."

"And?"

"And although I chose you, it's your opinion I consider you available, instead of special."

"Bingo!"

"On the other hand, *I'm* supposed to feel special even though you came here planning to sell your body to the first guy who made you a proper offer."

She slaps his face.

The surrounding customers jump back with nervous looks. But Jill seems more surprised than anyone.

"*Omigod!*" she says. "I'm so *sorry!*"

The bartender hurries over, all puffed up. "Say the word, Jill, and he's out of here."

"It's okay, Clarise. Please don't tell Mr. Ray."

Clarise says, "You're tellin' me this was *your* fault?"

"Yes," she says. "I don't know what got into me. I'm so sorry!"

Clarise looks at Jack. "You gonna complain?"

"Of course not!"

"What happened here, exactly?"

"I asked her what she'd do if a guy tried to grab her onstage, and she said she'd slap his face. I asked how hard, and she showed me."

Clarise chuckles. "Next time you'll think twice, huh?"

"Next time I will."

After Clarise moves away, Jill says, "Thanks."

Jack smiles. "You're a handful."

"I am. Don't forget it."

He says, "Can we move past all this?"

"Yes. Soon as you admit I'm right."

Jack sighs. "Suppose you *are* right about me, that I go from club to club and try to make women feel special. How does that make me worse than a guy who buys an hour of your time tonight and moves along to the next woman tomorrow?"

"Because that guy's being honest. He's not trying to put hope in my heart."

"What's wrong with hope?"

"Hope is like kindling. It makes you vulnerable. The smallest spark can burn your dreams to the ground."

He stares at her blankly.

Jill says, "You're trying to think of something clever to say, aren't you?"

"Possibly."

"Don't. And don't try to be charming, either."

"Why not?"

"I want you to be yourself."

"What if I'm naturally charming?"

"Then stop."

"Why?"

"Because I'm not finished being mad at you."

"Okay."

"Why would you even *offer* me such a ridiculous date?"

"Honestly? I thought you were extremely...um...*adorable*... and thought you'd appreciate being treated like a lady."

"Okay, so I know I said adorable a while ago, but that's too big a stretch. Next time you play Henry Higgins, call the older ones gorgeous. They'll eat it up like candy. As for wanting me to feel like a lady?"

"Yeah?"

"I guess it makes you feel like a big man, doesn't it? Turning a hooker into a lady? Well you know how it makes *me* feel?"

"How?"

"Like I'm a homeless, skid row gutter snipe, and you've tossed me a pastry. And if I show up at the same street corner on Monday, I might get another one."

"What's wrong with pastry?"

"I'll have no use for the fancy dress after Monday. Buying the damn thing sets a bad example for my daughters, who, by the way, will get their hopes up for nothing."

"What do you mean?"

"They'll be so excited watching me get all fixed up for the big date. They won't understand the whole thing's a sham. They'll send me off with high hopes, and I'll have to come home and tell them things didn't work out. Otherwise, they'll spend the next three days waiting for the phone and doorbell to ring."

"Why?"

"To see if my rich boyfriend, who took me to fucking Pirouette Restaurant, is going to call or send me flowers."

"And of course I won't do either."

"Of course you won't. At least you're admitting it."

"There's a perfectly good reason. And it's not because I don't *want* to call you or send you flowers."

"It's just that you're married."

"*What?*"

"You're married."

"I'm not married!"

"Then what?"

89

Jack smiles. "I don't have your phone number or address, remember?"

A few seconds pass, then Jill smiles.

"What?"

She makes a clucking sound.

Again, Jack says, "What?"

"I've been pretty rough on you."

"Ya think?"

She shakes her head. "I can't believe you're still here."

"Could it be I think you're special?"

"No," she says. Then laughs.

"Let's start over," Jack says. "Forget Le Pirouette. Where would *you* like to have dinner?"

"Seriously?"

He nods.

Jill says, "You know the Pancake House on Eighth and James?"

He laughs. "The Pancake House? Seriously?"

"You asked."

"I can find it. How's seven-thirty Monday evening?"

"I'll be there."

"See you then," Jack says, and leaves money for the drink that never came.

Chapter 5

Jill watches Jack carefully as he weaves his way through the crowd, toward the exit. She specifically wants to see if he makes eye contact with any of the girls, or if his eyes linger on their asses.

To her surprise, he pays no attention to the other girls.

It suddenly dawns on Jill he didn't even stay long enough to watch *her* routine.

What type of man comes into a place like this, meets a thirty-year-old hooker, shows her nothing but respect, offers to take her out on a real date, and gives her not one, but *two* thousand dollars in advance?

She knows the answer.

A complete sucker.

Jill's business thrives on suckers. It's a business completely dependent upon a woman's ability to separate men from their senses, knowing their wallets will follow.

Jill has no intention of meeting Jack at the Pancake House on Monday. From the moment he gave her the first envelope she knew he was ripe for the plucking. *Feign anger,* she thought. *Put him on the defensive.*

Works every time on nice guys.

There's the rub, of course.

Jack has the potential to be a genuinely nice guy.

There was a moment where she nearly caved. Contrary to what she told him, there's something about Jack that stirs her up inside and inspires hope. She could actually see herself falling for this guy. Then she realized he already had the envelopes in his pocket, which proves she wasn't special to him at all.

They say the nice guys are all married, but the truth is *all* guys are nice when they want something. The sad truth is, there *are* no nice guys. No Prince Charmings. Not here, not anywhere, and the only thing dumber than falling for a bullshit artist's spiel is falling for the bullshit artist himself.

She stares at the envelopes in her lap.

Two thousand dollars.

For doing absolutely nothing!

She briefly wonders if she's doing the right thing, dumping Jack before the first date. Could she play him for twice as much?

Probably not.

His move is to swoop in, make the grand gesture, convince himself he's on a date with a pretty lady instead of a hooker. He wines her, dines her, beds her, moves on to the next "conquest."

Why go to so much time and trouble to get laid by a hooker?

Lack of confidence. Fear of rejection. Fear of intimacy. Fear of commitment.

Jill tries to see it through Jack's eyes. He wants to feel like he's got a girlfriend. Wants to go out on a "real" date, but wants to be certain of the outcome. Wants to know his date will find him funny, charming, and witty. Wants the night to end with passionate sex.

For a guy like Jack, hookers are the ultimate "sure thing."

Doesn't mean he's a *bad* guy, just means he's not the right guy for her.

Still, she can't believe she's going to jilt him at such a ludicrous place.

The Pancake House!

What a sap!

She smiles, picturing the handsome, well-dressed Jack arriving early, waiting for her outside the restaurant. After a while he'll wonder if he got the time wrong. He'll go inside, search the tables. Then he'll go back outside to wait. Then he'll wonder if she entered while he was searching for her in the restaurant. Did she go in the ladies' room to check her makeup? If so, she might have gotten a table *after* he went back outside. So he'll go back in and check all the same tables a second time.

Who gets stood up by a hooker at a pancake restaurant?

It's funny, right?

At one point in her life she'd feel bad doing this to a guy. But tonight she tells herself it's the best thing that could happen to both of them. She needs the money and he needs a lesson. Two thousand bucks represents a new start. She can leave this shit job behind her, move to a big city like Louisville, reinvent herself. She's already got a fake ID. She's been using it with her day job for weeks. It'll be easy to slip into the Emma Wilson character when she gets to Louisville. Then maybe she can find a nice, wealthy guy who'll fall in love with her and treat her with the respect she deserves. Someone decent, and kind. Someone like...

Well, like Jack.

Except that it can't be Jack.

It can't be Jack because he knows her as a hooker. And no matter how well he treats her during the courtship, no matter how deeply he might fall in love with her, he'll never marry her. And even if by some miracle he did, he'd insist on a dreadful pre-nup, and the first time they fight, what'll come out of his mouth is, "When I met you, you were nothing but a fucking whore!"

And he'll be right.

Once a whore, always a whore.

So Jack's out.

But Jill can't help but wish someone else had given her the money tonight, and that when she moves to Louisville tomorrow, the first guy she meets could have been Jack.

She palms the envelopes, heads to her dressing room. Goes into the bathroom, enters a stall, locks the door. Takes a deep breath, opens the first envelope.

Her eyes grow huge. Her pulse pounds in her ears.

She gasps.

With trembling fingers, she tears open the second envelope.

And screams.

Chapter 6

The envelopes are full of newsprint. Dozens of newspaper pages, cut into strips the size of bills.

What the hell?

She re-runs it in her mind.

Jack never said "Here's a thousand dollars."

What he said was, "You'll need tires to drive to the restaurant."

When he gave her the second envelope he didn't say, "Use five hundred of this to buy yourself a dress."

What he said was, "Perhaps you can use this to buy a suitable dress."

Right.

And perhaps she can't.

Jill thought she was playing *him*, but it turns out *he* was playing *her*.

Toying with her.

But why?

She studies the strips of newsprint to see if he's written something on them.

He hasn't.

Could there be a message contained in the newsprint?

Ten minutes of careful review says no.

She storms out the bathroom, through the dressing area, climbs the steps to the back of the stage. Asks one of the girls, "Where's Brutus?"

"Outside," the dancer says, "grabbing a smoke."

She goes outside, calls his name.

Brutus stubs out his cigarette, walks over to her.

"What's up, Sugarpants?"

"You still owe me two hundred."

"Which I said I'd pay you next Friday," he says, with some attitude.

"You want to work it off in trade?"

"How?"

"I want you to beat up a guy for me."

"When?"

Jill lets out a laugh.

"What?"

"Most people would ask who, or why," she says. "You just want to know when."

"So?"

"I like that."

He waits.

"Monday night," she says. "Seven-fifteen."

"Where?"

"You know the Pancake House?"

"The one where you waitress?"

"Yeah. I'll meet you in the parking lot and point him out."

"This ain't a robbery, is it?"

"No. I just want him roughed up."

"It'll have to be quick. A couple to the face, couple to the ribs, maybe a kick or two when he's down. Twenty, thirty seconds, okay?"

"Okay."

"After that, we're square, right? On the two hundred?"

"Yeah."

"This ain't the guy you were talkin' to at the bar a few minutes ago, is it? The one you slapped?"

"Yeah. Why?"

"Guy had on a Brioni jacket."

"So?"

"Why would a guy like that go to a pancake house?"

"To meet me for dinner."

Brutus looks at her a moment, then shakes his head.

"What?"

"Women," he says.

He lights another cigarette, walks back to the employee smoking area.

Chapter 7

Monday Night.

"That's him," Jill says.

"No way," Brutus says.

"What's wrong?"

"Too many people."

"What if I walk him around the side of the building, by the dumpster?" she says.

"I don't know."

"What's the problem?"

"I didn't think there'd be this many people. What if he cries out?"

"What if he *does*?"

"I'm on probation, Jill."

"It's two hundred dollars for twenty seconds of work."

He looks around a minute, then says, "Okay. But if someone shows up, I walk. If I walk, we're still square on the two hundred."

"How do you figure that?"

"My time and effort."

"Walking away doesn't take much effort."

"My time, then."

She pauses a moment, then says, "Fine. Circle the building, wait by the dumpster, jump out when you see us."

They separate, and Jill crosses the parking lot to the front of the building, where Jack's waiting.

"Jill!" he says, enthusiastically. "I'm so glad you came!"

"You've got a lot of nerve!" she says.

"Let's go inside and talk about it," Jack says.

"Let's not."

"Why?"

"There's a good chance I'll raise my voice. What you did to me was the meanest thing I've ever seen. You knew I needed that money."

"If we can talk for just a minute..."

She pauses, then says, "Okay."

"Okay?"

"Yeah," Jill says. "Walk with me."

"Where?"

"Away from this dinner crowd."

"Lead the way."

She leads him around the building. As they turn the corner, he reaches into his pocket and hands her a thick envelope.

"This again?"

He sees her looking around.

She raises her voice and says, "Fool me once, shame on you. Fool me twice—"

"Shame on *me!*" Brutus yells, running toward them, full speed. He pushes Jack back into the building. When Jack tries to gain his footing, Brutus punches his left cheek, then his right eye, and follows it with a knee to the groin. Jack falls to the pavement, Brutus kicks him. Jack curls up into a fetal position. Brutus kicks him again.

Jack goes unconscious.

Brutus looks around, then nods at Jill.

She nods back.

He leaves.

Jill opens the envelope and says, "*Holy shit!*"

Chapter 8

Ten Minutes Earlier...

Jack checks his watch as Jill pulls into the Pancake House parking lot. He's in his car, across the street, where he's been for the past forty minutes. He watches her park as far as possible from the restaurant's front door. A couple minutes later Jack sees a large guy walk over to Jill's car.

He knows the guy.

Doesn't know his name, but recognizes him as one of the bouncers from Favors Strip Club. Jack's first thought is Jill might be in trouble. He fires up the car and drives across the street. But when he gets to the parking lot he decides they're having a friendly conversation. So either it's a helluva coincidence they'd run into each other at the Pancake House, or...

Or he's here to beat me up.

Jack decides to play it out, see what happens. He keeps his eyes forward, enters the lot, finds a parking space close to the entrance, then walks to the front door. A minute later, Jill walks over to him. She's wearing skinny jeans, an off-the-shoulder tunic, and looks amazing.

He greets her warmly.

Not surprisingly, she's furious. Doesn't want to go inside. Wants to walk around the building to talk.

Jack looks for the big guy, but doesn't see him. He walks with her around the building, ninety percent certain he's about to get pummeled.

He gives Jill the envelope stuffed with hundred dollar bills.

Fifty of them.

Five grand.

That's got to please her.

Except she doesn't believe him, because he shafted her the first time. She's looking around, saying something about fooling her once. And...

Showtime!

Jack sees him coming and has to make a quick decision. Should he run? Fight? Or accept the beating?

He chooses to accept the beating.

It's over quickly.

Jack pretends he's out cold.

Will she walk over to see if he's okay?

No. She's opening the envelope. And likes what she sees inside. Finally, she walks over to check on him.

It's not exactly Romeo and Juliet, but it's a start, right?

Something to build on.

Chapter 9

"Jack! Are you okay?" she says, shamelessly.

"Huh?" he says, pretending to come around.

"You've been attacked! I'll call an ambulance."

"No. I'll be fine."

"Fine? Are you crazy? You're bleeding!"

She helps him sit up.

"I'll go in the bathroom, get cleaned up," he says. "Then we can have dinner like we planned."

"Not here," she says.

"Why not?"

She breaks eye contact, and sighs. "I work here."

"*What?*"

"During the day."

"Seriously?"

She pauses, then says, "The truth is, I wasn't planning to meet you tonight "

"I don't understand."

She takes a deep breath. "I set you up."

"With the big guy?"

"Yeah. I'm sorry. I was angry with you."

"You had every right."

"I agree," she says. "Why would you *do* that? Give me envelopes filled with newspaper?"

"One reason is I was afraid someone would steal it from you. But the real reason is I thought you might use it to leave town."

"I can't believe you thought that!"

"Well, I didn't really know you that well."

"What made you think I'd show up after getting stiffed?"

"I was counting on you being angry enough to come tell me off."

"At which point you give me the two thousand dollars?"

"There's five thousand, actually."

"No shit?"

"Count it."

"I don't understand."

"I like you, Jill."

"*Did* like me, you mean."

"Still do. I think."

"Even though I paid someone to beat you up?"

"Yeah. I think so."

She helps him to his feet, props him against the wall. "Are you okay to walk?"

"One way to find out."

He takes a couple of shaky steps, winces, then leans against the building for support.

"How much did you pay him?" Jack says.

"Two hundred bucks."

"You got your money's worth."

She smiles. "You've got a very forgiving nature."

"Thanks. Where do you want to eat?"

"My place."

"What about your girls?"

She shakes her head. "I don't have any kids, Jack."

"You don't?"

Chapter 10

Christ, what a rube, Jill thinks.

She doesn't know how it happened, but one thing she's learned over the years, chemistry between two people can't be predicted. Another thing she's learned is a man will pay his last nickel to possess what he truly wants. And what Jack wants is for Jill to want *him*. Buying her body appears to hold no interest for him. He literally said what he wanted the very first minute they spoke.

He wants her to be his girlfriend.

Why?

Who gives a shit! He's already paid five grand for the privilege, and she hasn't given up so much as a kiss! If she handles it right, Jack'll give her another five before the evening's over.

"I should get my car," Jill says.

"I'll follow you home," he says. "That way you won't have to drive me back here after dinner."

"Nonsense," she says. "You're in no condition to drive."

"That's probably true," he says.

"Wait here. I'll get my car and bring it to you."

"Are you going to ditch me?"

"No." She flashes a warm smile. "I promise."

A minute later her car pulls up. She helps him get in.

"You sure you don't want to go to the emergency room?" Jill says. "You might have a concussion."

"I'm fine. Just a little shaken up, is all."

"I'm really sorry about that."

"Please. It was my fault."

She looks at the expression on his face and everything changes. *Forget the plan, forget the money*, she tells herself. Some things are more important. Like recognizing a good man when he's an arm's length away. *I've been an idiot, a fool*, she realizes. *But no more! From now on it's going to be no lies, no bullshit.*

Just Jill.

What changed her mind?

This man's a prize. He's worth fighting for, worth trusting. He's worth her finest effort.

She takes his hand, brings it to her lips, kisses it.

"You're a good man," she says.

"But not a better person than you," he says, smiling. "Remember telling me that at the club? I still agree with you."

She says, "If we're being honest, you're a much better person than I am."

She starts the car and gasps. Looks down, trying to fathom what caused the sharp pain in her thigh. Sees Jack holding a hypodermic needle. Feels a cold rush as the liquid fills her bloodstream and makes her so groggy she can't put the car in gear. She tries to reach down, pull the needle from her thigh, but has no control over her hand. Her eyelids grow heavy. She feels her body going slack. Works to form a single word.

Why?

But can't.

Jill wants to explain she was planning to take him home, give him what he wanted. She was going to open her heart, take a chance on him. But even if it turned out he didn't want her, she still fully intended to make sure he left her house happy and satisfied tonight. Because while two grand would have given her a new start, five grand gives her a new life.

And speaking of the five grand?

She remains conscious long enough to see him put the cash envelope and her Emma Wilson driver's license in his jacket pocket.

Chapter 11

"Where are we?" Jill says, in a voice made thick from the drug.

"Memphis," Jack says.

"Why?"

"Think about it."

Jill wants to scratch his eyes out, grab him by the throat, strangle him to death. But she'll settle for grabbing the car keys and trying to make a run for it.

Except she can't.

Her wrists are above her head, handcuffed to the headrest.

What about her feet? Maybe she can kick him till he pulls over or crashes into something. But no, her feet are bound with his belt, and hooked to something below the seat that restricts her movement.

"I need to pee," she says.

Jack laughs. 'There it is. The go-to comment."

"What do you mean?"

"They always say that."

"Who?"

"Women. When they're trapped. It's the first thing they say."

"You've trapped a lot of women in your life?"

"Transported is a better word."

"What is it you *do*, exactly, Jack?"

"I'm a bounty hunter."

"You're joking."

"Dead serious, actually."

"What does that have to do with *me*?"

Jack says nothing.

Jill says, "I really *do* need to pee."

Jack says, "No one's stopping you from peeing, Jill."

Chapter 12

"Where are we?" Jill says, coming around for the second time.

"Hour north of Jackson, Mississippi."

"Why?"

"Think about it."

"You're taking me back. To La Pierre, Louisiana."

They ride in silence a few minutes before Jill says, "How much is he paying you?"

"That's confidential."

"Please don't take me back," she says. "I'll do anything."

"So you say."

"Name it, Jack. Anything you want."

"Look at me."

She does.

He says, "This business about you being a hooker? It's bullshit."

She starts to say something, changes her mind. Then says, "What tipped you off?"

"Friday night. Favors Strip Club."

"What about it?"

"You didn't ask me to buy you a drink."

She thinks a minute, then says, "Is that such a big deal?"

"Big enough to set you apart from every bar hooker in the history of the world."

"And yet I would have had sex with you. And still would, if you'll agree to let me go."

"That wasn't your only mistake."

"What else?"

"You asked me to set the price. Again, that's a first."

"You've obviously had a lot of experience with prostitutes. Your mother must be very proud."

"My mother was a prostitute. She wouldn't be proud, but she wouldn't be judgmental, either. As for your other mistakes? You got mad because I didn't make you feel special. Do I really need to tell you hookers don't expect a special relationship? And they don't insult potential customers. Also, you grabbed the seat beside me too quickly. It reeked of desperation."

"That's unique among hookers?"

"Sadly, no. But with your looks, it's a bad move."

"Why?"

"Of all the women in the club, you're the prize."

"That's ridiculous. Most of them are little more than half my age."

"Those girls are cute or pretty at best. You're beautiful. Refined. Clean. And you're not on drugs. You're mysterious."

"Mysterious? How?"

"Because you never let the customers see you completely naked on stage. You're the one they'd pay big money to bang, but it has to be their idea, not yours. Friday night I could have had you for a fraction of what you're worth."

The dashboard light casts a green glow across Jill's face. Jack starts a mental ten-count. By the time he gets to three, she asks the question he knew was coming.

"How much *am* I worth?"

"You're too high class to turn tricks. You could be a courtesan."

"Which is what, exactly?"

"Top of the line. A companion. With benefits."

"Define high class. In terms of a hooker."

"She's beautiful. Smart. Classy. Sexy. She'll fit in wherever a wealthy guy wants to take her."

"And that's worth how much?"

"Three grand for a night, five for a weekend, ten for a week."

"And if I were ten years younger?"

"Twice that."

"Is that what *you* pay high class hookers?"

He pauses a moment, then says, "Let's talk about you."

"What about me?"

"I knew before I met you."

"Knew what?"

"That you never turned a trick in your life. That you only started stripping three weeks ago, and can't even finance your buy-in because you've been lending money to the bouncers and dancers, trying to fit in. That's a rookie move, by the way. They were taking advantage of you. Beyond that, you're not a real stripper. You move well, but never go past pasties and panties."

"You've been watching me?"

He nods.

"How long?"

"In the club? Couple of times. All together? A month, give or take."

"Where?"

"Your apartment, the club, your day job, your errands, job interviews."

"You knew I worked at the Pancake House?"

"Of course. Speaking of which, would you prefer I call you Emma Wilson?"

She ignores the question, saying, "You knew I kept flunking job interviews?"

"I knew."

"Then you knew how desperate I was."

"Which is why I stepped in when I did."

"You knew I was ready to sell my body?"

"I knew you were getting close. And I didn't want that for you."

"You've been following me around for a month?"

"About that."

"Why'd you wait so long before taking me back?"

Jack starts to reply, but she cuts him off, saying, "Wait, I know. You were building your fee. Pretending you couldn't find me right away."

He shrugs. She's wrong, but does it really make a difference?

Chapter 13

Jill drifts in and out of sleep as the effects of the drug slowly wear off. At one point she asks, "You got any kids?"

"No."

They go silent again, until he says, "What made you ask that?"

She shrugs. "Your name's Jack. At least that's what you told me."

"It's Jack. So what?"

"We passed Jackson a while ago. Made me wonder. You know, Jack's *son?*"

He says nothing.

Jill says, "Not a fan of word play, I take it."

"Why'd you run off?"

She groans, rolls her eyes. "*Seriously*, Jack? You're smart enough to track me down, but don't know why I left?"

"Your husband, Bobby Dee. The mobster."

"*Monster's* a better description."

She sees him glance at her, so she adds, "You're wondering how bad it could have been. And I'd tell you if I thought it would change your mind."

"Can't hurt," he says.

"Yeah, it can."

"How?"

"It'll give you more information to use against me. Fatten your fee."

"You think I'd do that?"

"We're here, aren't we?"

"I'm just doing my job."

"Calling it your job doesn't make it right."

"We saw what *you* were willing to do Friday night to pay the bills."

"Yes, we did. And thanks for reminding me how you really see me."

This is exactly why she can never let herself fall for Jack. He'll never forget she was willing to sell her body.

"My life was literally on the line," she says. "I knew I couldn't stay there much longer without getting caught. I was about to be kicked out of my apartment. I was down to my last tank of gas."

"What about the Pancake House job?"

"I'm still working off the advance they gave me."

"So you decided to sell your body."

"To you, Jack. To *you*. Not the next person who happened by. You think you're the first guy who came in the bar last Friday? I chose *you!*"

"Why?"

"Same things you said about me. You're great-looking. You're clean. You're a cut above. I felt if I had to trade sex for money just this once, I could live with myself if I did it with someone like you. And I'm still willing to, if you'll let me go. Like you said, I'm not a hooker. I've slept with exactly five men in my entire life. But I'll give you all I've got, Jack. You can do whatever you want to me, and toss me in a ditch when you're through. I'll still be better off. Just...*please, Jack!*"

"What?"

"Don't take me back to Bobby!"

Jack says nothing, keeps driving, eyes straight ahead.

"If you know my husband at all, you know he's a sick, sadistic bastard. He's going to brutalize me for running away. He might very well kill me. And you're delivering me to his doorstep. I thought I saw something in you, Jack. But if you take me back, you're no better than him."

"I don't abuse women."

"But you'll willingly take me to a man who does! Bobby's going to physically assault me in every sick and twisted way you can imagine. He's going to rape me. Beat me. Punish me. Chain me to a wall. Deprive me of food, water, sleep. He's going to humiliate me a hundred different ways till he breaks me down and destroys my will to live. He won't stop till my last ounce of dignity is gone. And when he's finally tired of abusing me, he's going to..." her voice trails off in the air.

"He's going to what?"

"I can't say it."

"Why not?"

"If you tell him I said it, he'll kill you."

Jack looks at her with curiosity. "You'd care if he kills me?"

"Of *course* I'd care!"

"Why?"

"Are you serious?"

She gives him a look that combines several emotions at once. Anger. Fear. Sadness...

She says, "You're all I've got, Jack. You're my only hope."

She stares at him ten full minutes, but receives nothing in return. Finally she says, "I *need* you, Jack. He'll *kill* me. You *know* he will."

"Correct me if I'm wrong," he says, "but you were desperate for money, right?"

"You know I was."

"Couldn't pay your rent, down to your last tank of gas."

"That's right."

"And yet you paid a bouncer two hundred bucks to beat me up."

"Jack! That was—"

"That was a spiteful thing to do. And you know *why* you did it? To punish me. So tell me again why I should care if your husband punishes *you*?"

Jill wants to explain Brutus the bouncer wasn't going to repay her anyway, so it didn't really *cost* her anything. But that wouldn't change the fact she wanted to punish Jack for shafting her. She could try to explain her heart skipped a beat when she saw him enter the club Friday night, that she found him crazy handsome, and that just when it seemed he'd solved all her problems, he shit all over her by giving her newsprint instead of cash. But none of that matters, because even though it's all true, she never intended to show up for the date. She was planning to take his money and run. And when he shafted her, she did, in fact, want to punish him.

But there's a difference between her and Bobby when it comes to punishment.

Bobby won't limit her beating to twenty seconds.

He's going to torture her, then feed her to the wild hogs he keeps in a pen on the Blood River.

She notices the car slowing down.

"What are you doing?" she says.

"Pulling over."

"Why?"

Chapter 14

"We need gas," Jack says.

"We're in the middle of nowhere."

"There are eight gas cans in the trunk. Forty gallons."

"What are you *talking* about? This is my car. There are no gas cans in the trunk."

"I switched them from my trunk to yours at the restaurant. While you were unconscious."

Jack gets out, opens the trunk, starts filling the tank.

"Can I pee?" she hollers.

He drains the first tank and tosses it twenty feet into the field beside them. Then he circles the car, opens the door, and says, "Please don't try anything stupid."

Two sets of cuffs secure her wrists to the metal base of the headrest. Jack removes them, along with the belt binding her feet. He takes her by the hand, leads her ten yards into the field.

"Can you give me some privacy?" she says.

"It's pitch black. I couldn't see you if I tried."

"Can you at least turn away?"

"Yeah, I can do that. But I'm keeping my hand on your head."

"Why?"

"Just deal with it."

She squats, pulls her pants down. He holds her in place, turns away. The sound of her peeing reminds him he's due. When she's done he says, "Sit tight."

He unzips his pants, pees in the opposite direction.

"This is weird," she says.

"Can't be helped. Thanks for not trying to run."

"Where would I go?"

"Still. Thanks."

"You're welcome."

He finishes, zips his fly. Sees two pick-up trucks pulling off the road. They come to a stop behind Jill's car.

Jack crouches beside her. Whispers, "Keep quiet."

"Promise you'll let me go."

"I can't do that, Jill."

She screams.

Chapter 15

Four doors open, four men get out. One has a spotlight in his hands, the others, rifles. All are illuminated by the trucks' headlights and flashers.

Jack assesses the situation. Four redneck deer hunters, three rifles, thirty feet away.

It takes two seconds for the spotlight to find them.

"That was a stupid thing to do," Jack whispers.

"You gave me no choice," Jill says.

"These guys are bad news."

"Whatever happens, I'll be better off."

One of the hunters says, "Holy shit! Looky what we got here! I think my birthday done come early!"

Jill whispers, "Sorry Jack, but I can't go back to La Pierre." To the men she yells, "Please help me!"

"What's goin' on here, little lady?" one of the men calls out.

"This man kidnapped me. I fear for my life."

"*Kidnapped* you?"

"Yes, sir."

"What do you think, boys?"

"I call first fuck!" one says.

"I call second!" says another.

"I'll go third, then," says a third.

First guy says, "Guess you're fourth on the list, Clem."

Clem says, 'Well, I'm willin' to fuck the girl while waitin' my turn."

Jack and Jill look at each other.

The first hunter yells, "Stand up, put your hands in the air."

Jack types some keys on his cell phone.

"You're making a *phone* call?" Jill whispers.

"Shield your eyes," Jack says.

One of the men fires a shot that hisses into the grass five feet from Jack's position.

"*Now!*" he yells. "Hands in the—"

His words are drowned out by the explosion, as Jill's trunk becomes a fireball. Jack pulls a gun from his ankle holster and shoots two of the men before they can react. The other two are human torches, running into the field, screaming, falling down, rolling on the ground. Jack grabs Jill by the wrist and takes her where the men are on the ground, writhing in pain.

He stands over them, empties his gun.

Jill screams.

"I'm sorry you had to see that," he says.

"Fuck *that*," she says. "You blew up my *car?*"

"Yeah."

"How?"

"I wired it earlier. Just in case."

"When did you have time to do that?"

"It's just a blasting cap and plastic explosive. And a receiver."

"You couldn't possibly have known this would happen."

"No. But it was my insurance in case Bobby decided to kill me."

"Why would he kill *you?*"

"For doing this."

He takes her in his arms and kisses her. She tries to pull away, yells, "*Stop* it!"

As the flame from the car crackles and roars in the background, Jack releases his grip.

"I thought it's what you wanted," he says.

"I was willing to make an *investment* in you," she says. "And still am. But only if you promise to let me go."

"I can't."

"Why not?"

He sighs. "Because we can't run away together unless you're divorced or Bobby's dead. He's got too many resources. He'd find us."

"You've thought about it. About us running away together."

"I've thought about nothing else for the better part of a month."

"Then let's do it! It's the only way. He'll never give me a divorce."

Jack says nothing.

Jill says, "You *have* thought about something else. You've thought about killing him."

"It crossed my mind."

"Uncross it, Jack. He's got an army of security people, and the house is a fortress."

"I had a nice diversion planned."

"The car bomb?"

"Uh huh."

"Wouldn't have worked."

"Probably not. Doesn't matter. I watched you day and night for weeks, Jill. Watched and wanted you till I ached. In my head I created this dream where you and I could be together. I dreamed we'd kill Bobby, take what money we could find, run away to my safe place."

"What safe place?"

"I've got a lake house in a little town called Willow Lake, in the Ozarks. My retirement spot."

"You're awfully young to be thinking about retirement."

"Doesn't mean I can't enjoy it while waiting to grow old."

"Then why don't we just go there?"

"When we got together for dinner tonight you made it clear your interest in me was zero."

"Because you shafted me, Jack."

"We've been through this already. The bottom line is you don't give a shit about me. You just want to get away."

"Not true," she says. "Look. I won't pretend I *love* you, and the truth is I didn't even *like* you till just now, when I saw how you handled this situation. But I'm willing to give you a chance. Forget trying to kill Bobby. That's suicide. But I'm willing to go with you to your safe place right now. No promises, but I'll give it an honest try. How about it?"

"I guess for you it's better than being with Bobby."

"Much better. Let's do it, Jack. Run away to your place. I'll make it worth your while."

"How?"

She moves closer, finds his lips.

As they kiss, she grabs his hand, slides it under her bra, falls on her back. He leans over her, exposes her breasts. He can't see them, but his hands and mouth have no problem finding them. Her nipples feel longer and harder than they could possibly be, and to his joy he hears her pulling her pants down. He slides lower, kisses her stomach. Slides his body lower still, so he can reach her sweet spot. Feels his foot touch one of the dead, smoldering rednecks, and kicks the corpse out of his way.

"Let's escape, Jack," she says. "You and me. We'll start a new life. Say you'll do it!"

"I'll do it."

"Oh, thank *God!*" she says.

He moves upward, kisses her lips. Starts unzipping his pants, says, "Shit!"

"You *came* already?"

"No."

"Then what?"

"We've got company."

She tilts her head, sees the flashing lights of a police car as it pulls off the road and comes to a stop in front of Jill's burning car.

"Let me handle this," she says.

"Okay."

Chapter 16

Jack and Jill adjust their clothing, and meet the state trooper as he comes around the front of his car. Jill moves forward and tells him she and Jack stopped to put gas in their car, and the two trucks pulled up and four men got out with rifles and threatened to rape them.

"They threatened to rape *both* of you?" he says.

"Mostly him " she says.

She tells him Jack fired a warning shot that must have hit the gas cans in the trunk, causing them to blow up. "Then Jack shot the men," she says. "In self-defense."

He nods.

"Does that make sense?" she says.

He nods again.

"Do you need to take down our statements or anything?"

He shakes his head, no.

"There are four bodies here, officer. But everything that happened was self-defense."

He nods.

"You believe me, don't you?"

He nods again.

"So is that it? We're free to go? Why aren't you saying anything?"

He raises his chin, indicating Jack. She turns, sees him aiming his gun at the policeman's head.

"How long have you been holding a gun on him?" Jill asks.

"From the moment you stepped in front of me."

"Why?"

"Because there's no way he's going to allow this to sit without calling for backup, checking the scene, taking us to the station, getting all in our business."

"You can't just shoot him. He's a cop."

"I'm not going to shoot unless he forces me."

"What happens next?"

"I'm going to tell him what's really going on."

"What's wrong with my story?"

"Tell her," he says to the cop.

"Gas tanks don't explode from gunshots, Miss. That only happens on TV."

"And?" Jack says.

"And you've identified yourself as a witness to a quadruple homicide. And implicated your friend here, as the killer."

Jack says, "We're lucky he didn't see the bodies before getting out of the car. Otherwise he would've radioed for help."

"Actually, I *did* call it in," the policeman says.

"Then you'll need to radio again."

"Why would I do that?"

"I'm Jack Tallow. This is Jill DiPiese, Bobby DiPiese's wife. He hired me to find her, bring her back."

Jill says, "I don't believe you're doing this. What about our plans—"

Jack puts his fingers to his lips and says, "It's the only way."

He reaches into his pocket, pulls out a card, hands it to the officer. Then he gets his cell phone out, presses a button on it, waits a moment, and says, "Mr. Dee, this is Jack Tallow. We've got a situation."

Chapter 17

Bobby DiPiese's gone by the name Bobby Dee for so long, he can barely remember how to spell his surname. Four hours ago he was happy as a priest with two peckers when he heard Tallow had found his wife, and was bringing her in.

"Call me two minutes before you get here," he said. "We'll open the garage door. You'll pull in, we'll shut the door behind you. And keep quiet. I don't want anyone to know about this business with Jill."

Now Tallow's calling from south of Kentwood, saying they pulled over to put some gas in the car and had to kill four rednecks and set Jill's car on fire. Worse, he had to tell a state trooper he was bringing Jill in, which totally fucks up Bobby's plans for dealing with his errant wife. Unless...

"Who's the trooper?" he asks.

He hears Jack say, "What's your name?"

The cop says, "Henry Gauthiereaux."

Bobby smiles.

Jack says, "Did you hear him, Mr. Dee?"

"I heard. Put Officer Hank on the phone."

Chapter 18

Jack and Jill sit tight as the arrangements are worked out between Bobby and Officer Hank.

"Would you have shot him?" Jill whispers.

"No way. I was bluffing," he whispers back.

"Because he's a state trooper?"

"Because I was out of bullets."

She can't tell if he's kidding.

Officer Hank looks at Jack, hands him the phone, says, "Your turn."

Jack puts the phone to his ear. Bobby says, "Grab one of the pickup trucks and haul ass out of there. Officer Hank's gonna wait at the scene. His story is he saw flames, drove up to investigate, found a car on fire, a parked pickup truck, and four dead men. End of story. He'll let the crime scene investigators draw the conclusions."

"Sounds good."

Bobby says, "Three people know Jill's been found. You, me, and Officer Hank, who's gonna retire a wealthy man if he keeps his mouth shut."

"Okay," Jack says. "I'm on my way."

"With Jill, of course."

"Of course."

Jack clicks the phone off, takes a step toward Jill, and all hell breaks loose.

"*Hit the ground and cover up!*" Jack yells, as a dozen shots ring out, simultaneously.

"Jesus!" Jill shouts.

"Who's shooting?" Officer Hank yells.

"I don't know!" Jack shouts.

But he does know. The flames in Jill's car have found his ammunition.

When the shots finally stop, Jill calls out, "Are you all right?"

"I'm good," Jack says. "You?"

"Yes. Is it over?"

"I think so."

He gets up, notices Officer Hank's chest bleeding in two places.

"Shit."

"What now?" Jill says.

"Officer Hank's dead."

"Check to make sure."

Jack clicks his cell phone on so he can use the screen light to illuminate Hank's face. When he puts it close, he jumps back, startled to find Hank very much alive.

"Get the fuck out of here!" Hank hisses.

"You need help," Jack says.

"I'll be fine. Now drive away, before you fuck up my retirement."

"Okay. Good luck."

"Fuck you both."

Chapter 19

"Wait a minute!" Jill says. "You're taking me to *Bobby*? After what just happened between us?"

They're in one of the pickups, thirty miles north of Hammond, ninety miles from Bobby's plantation outside La Pierre, Louisiana. Jack's driving, Jill's in the front seat.

"He'll *kill* me!" she says.

"I won't let that happen."

"He tortures people in the basement."

"I thought they didn't have basements in south Louisiana. It's below sea level, right?"

"Our home's on higher ground."

"Are you certain there's a basement?"

"According to Bobby there is. He used to threaten me. Said there's a secret entrance, a private underground area that goes back to the slave days. He said he puts people in there and tortures them. And that's what would happen to me if I ever ran away."

"Sounds like bullshit."

"What about the wild hogs?"

"Hogs?"

"He's got a pack of wild hogs penned up near the Blood River. He tortures people, crushes their legs, dumps them in the hog pen. The hogs tear them apart and eat them."

"That's ridiculous."

"You think?"

"Yes. But just to be sure, I'll stay on his good side."

"He doesn't *have* a good side, Jack. He's a stone killer. And he *owns* the police and politicians, as you just found out."

"He might own Officer Hank and a few others, but—"

"Jack, listen to me. We're free. Don't go to La Pierre. Drive to Baton Rouge. We'll ditch the truck at the airport and have a cab take us to Dallas. We'll catch a flight to—where's your lake house, Missouri? Arkansas?"

"Arkansas."

"Whatever. Let's get the hell away from Bobby."

"We can't afford to piss him off at this point."

"What do you mean 'at this point?'"

"We just left a murder scene. If Bobby finds out we've run off together, he'll call Officer Hank and have him turn us in."

"We'll be long gone by then."

"We can't outrun their radio. If they put out an APB on this truck, they'll catch us within an hour, put me in jail, and turn you over to Bobby. And I won't be able to protect you.

He might keep you alive till you testify against me, but after that, who knows?'"

"I don't *believe* this! We've got something special here, Jack. Don't take me back there!"

"It'll be okay, trust me. This is something I'm really good at. When we get there, I'll figure out a way to save you."

"He's got a half-dozen security guys in the house at all times."

"That's all?"

She frowns. "This is no time to act tough, Jack. All of Bobby's goons could wipe their ass with Brutus."

"Who's Brutus?"

"The bouncer who beat you up."

Jack laughs. "You think I couldn't have handled Brutus?"

"Oh, please. I was there. He knocked you out cold. You couldn't even walk."

Jack shakes his head in disbelief.

Jill says, "There's no shame in it, Jack. Brutus is huge. He fights for a living. All I'm saying, Bobby's goons are much tougher."

"I'll keep that in mind."

She says, "Are you seriously planning to take me back to Bobby?"

He sighs. "Much as I hate to, yeah."

"Then do me a favor."

"What?"

"Find a quiet place to make love to me."

"Don't tempt me."

"I'm serious."

"We're on a pretty tight schedule. I'd have to cum awfully quick."

"That won't be a problem."

"You think?"

"Sex is something *I'm* really good at, Jack."

Chapter 20

Turns out Jill's right. The entire event takes less than five minutes. Including pulling over, stopping the car, reclining the passenger seat, removing the clothing, doing it, putting the clothes back on, raising the seat, getting back on the highway.

"I'm embarrassed," Jack says.

"Don't be. It's just biology."

"That's the shortest biology lesson I've ever had," he says.

"I'll take that as a compliment."

As they approach the Hammond exit, Jack says, "What made you do that?"

"Have sex?"

"Yeah."

"I wanted us to bond."

"It worked."

She says, "If Bobby decides to spare your life, maybe you'll remember making love to me. Maybe you'll want to do it again."

"Count on it."

"Maybe you'll find a way to come back and save me."

"And if I don't?"

"I'll have the satisfaction of knowing I cheated on Bobby, which is *his* specialty."

"But you *wanted* to do it, right?"

"Of course! Why would you ask me that?"

"It sort of sounded like you were manipulating me."

"Seriously?"

"A little."

"I'll make you a deal."

"Tell me."

"Get me away from Bobby and I'll manipulate you in a way that'll put a permanent smile on your face."

"No problem. But I think you've got way too much respect for that old man."

"I lived with him, remember?"

"Yeah. But I'm trying to put it out of my mind."

"Me, too, Jack."

"What is he, sixty?"

"Yes. But don't sell him short. He's lethal."

"So am I."

"I hope so, Jack. Wait. Why are you turning here?"

"I've got an idea."

Chapter 21

Instead of heading south on 55, Jack takes the exit toward Hammond.

"We're going to rent a truck," he says. "U-Haul, Penske, whatever they've got."

"Whatever *who's* got?"

"The fine folks in Hammond."

"What's wrong with *this* truck?"

"Bobby knows we've got it. So does Officer Hank. We'll need gas soon, and it's only a matter of time before the investigating police realize another truck was at the crime scene."

"You don't think we'll be in La Pierre by then?"

"We're not going to La Pierre."

Jill looks up. "What do you mean?"

"Change of plans. We're going to Willow Lake."

"But—"

"Details to follow."

He hands her his cell phone. "Let me know when you get internet service."

She presses a few buttons. "We've got service right here."

"Good. Find us a truck rental company."

"It's eleven-thirty at night!"

"This is a small town. Someone will have an emergency number listed, or a home phone number. Or maybe they live above the store. I'm betting we'll get lucky."

"And if not?"

"We'll wake someone up and buy their car."

"What'll we use for money?"

"I've still got the five grand I stole back from you."

"Would *you* sell your family vehicle for five grand?"

"No, but I'd lend it to someone for a thousand bucks. And they will, too."

"And if they don't?"

"Then we'll steal their car."

"Are you for real?"

"You want to get away, right?"

"More than anything."

"I'm taking you to Willow Lake."

"Don't tease me."

"Call the truck places. We're going to Arkansas. Tonight. The more I think about it, the more I'm convinced we've got a fighting chance."

"Because?"

"I was very careful buying the land. I did it over time, under a separate identity. Then waited years before building the house. When it was time, I used an out-of-state construction crew."

"What identity have you been using there?"

"Don't laugh."

"Okay."

"Jack Russell."

She laughs.

He says, "It's a name everyone remembers. Who'd make up a name like that?"

"Good point."

"If we're super careful, Bobby might not find us."

"Please Jack. I'm taking this very seriously. Don't tease me."

"I'm not."

"Then bless your heart!"

She smiles broadly, then fusses with the phone keys a minute. Then says, "I've found five listings."

He leans over, kisses her cheek. "I'm sorry, Jill."

"For what?"

"Drugging you. Kidnapping you. Being a lousy lover..."

"Here's the great part: you'll have lots of opportunities to make it up to me."

"Especially the last part?"

"Especially that. Assuming we survive the night."

"Call the truck places. Maybe we'll get lucky."

She does, but they don't. Get lucky, that is.

Jack says. "Check the GPS to see which one's closest."

After a moment, she says, "Foster's Hardware."

Jill navigates, Jack drives. When they get to Foster's parking lot, he points to the house next door and says, "Perfect!"

"Why?"

"That's his house. I guarantee it."

"Who's?"

"Mr. Foster, of course."

"The same Mr. Foster who's going to blow our heads off with his shotgun?" she says.

"These are country people. They'll help us."

"What country are *you* from, crazy man?"

"Stay put," he says.

He turns off the engine, crosses the yard, climbs the porch steps, rings the doorbell.

Somewhere down the road a dog barks.

Then another.

And a third.

Jack rings the bell again.

A shadow moves quickly across the door. Before Jack can turn around and say, *What the hell?* a fist crashes into the base of his skull. He goes down in a heap, tries to scramble to his feet, but his equilibrium is off, and he falls back down. Sees a man preparing to kick him in the face, but also sees Jill coming up behind the guy with something in her hand. Something big, and heavy. Jack turns away from the kick and absorbs a glancing blow, but it's enough to make him see stars. When he attempts to stand, he's toppled by the guy who just kicked him, who's been knocked cold by Jill.

"Are you okay?" she says.

"Never better!"

She laughs at his aplomb, pulls the guy off him, and says, "Omigod, he's just a kid!"

"Kid?" Jack says. "This guy's a professional boxer."

"Don't be silly. Look at him. He can't be more than fifteen."

Jack gets to his feet, stares at the kid in disbelief. "I'll grant you he's young, but he's huge. And anyway, I think he hit me with a baseball bat."

"Of course he did."

The door suddenly bursts open, knocking Jack off-balance. His heel catches the porch step, and he falls backward, onto the sidewalk. A little old lady comes flying out the door, jumps on Jack and starts beating him with a rolling pin. He covers up, tries to buck her off, but she's got her knees dug into his sides, and she's spry. After raining countless blows on his arms, Jill steps in and hits her over the head the same way she hit the kid a moment ago.

Jack scrambles to his feet, drags the kid and old lady into the house, and turns on the lights. They're in a small parlor. To the left is the kitchen. Laundry room's to the right, hallway's in the center. Hallway leads to the bedrooms and bath.

"What did you hit them with?" Jack says.

She holds up a jack handle.

"From the truck?"

"Uh huh."

Jack says, "See if you can find something to tie them up."

She heads to the kitchen, hears Jack shout, "Fuck!" and comes back to find a shriveled old man hitting Jack over the head with a cane. She throws herself into the old man's knees.

He goes down and hits his head on the floor hard enough to knock him unconscious.

"Jesus, Jack!"

"What?"

"Is there *anyone* you can beat up?"

"What are you *talking* about?"

"Brutus?"

"I wanted to see what you were up to."

"The little old man?"

"I didn't want to hurt him."

"The little old lady?"

"Same thing."

"The grandson?"

"Lucky punch."

She crosses the floor, picks up the jack handle and says, "*You* find something to tie them up with. I'll stand guard."

Chapter 22

Jack and Jill stand over the squirming bodies, surveying their work.

"What now?" she says.

"We take their car."

"Whoa," Jill says.

She motions Jack to follow her into the kitchen. When he does, she lowers her voice so the Fosters can't hear. "We can't just *leave* them here. Sooner or later they'll get loose, call the cops, report their car stolen. Plus, they've seen us. They can identify us."

"Any suggestions?"

"Unless you're prepared to kill them, we'll need to put them in the trunk and take them with us."

"They could die in the trunk. Assuming they fit."

"They'll be fine till we get to the Baton Rouge airport."

"Then what?"

"We'll park in long-term. Then we walk away from the car, pop the trunk from a distance, and never look back.

We'll catch a cab to Memphis, catch another cab from there to Willow Lake."

"Memphis is out of the way."

"True. But that'll make it harder for Bobby to track us down."

"I like the way you think," Jack says. "Let's see if we can find the car keys."

"And the car."

"Right."

The car turns out to be an eleventh-generation Oldsmobile Ninety-Eight. A classic.

"We're in luck," Jack says.

"Why?"

"Oldsmobile made eleven versions of the Ninety-Eight. The final version was produced between 1991 and 1996. This model had nine more inches of trunk space."

"Thanks, Mr. Wizard," Jill says. "What I want to know is will it hold three coon asses?"

"I think so."

"Then help me carry them."

Jack gives her a mock salute.

When the bodies are loaded, he says, "If you need to use the bathroom, do it now."

"I'm good. How about you?"

"Give me a sec."

He goes to the kitchen, finds some paper and a pen, writes something on two pieces of paper, gives them to her.

"What's this, a love letter?"

"Even better. The first page has my cell phone number, lake house address, and describes my cover story. I'm a builder, from Saint Louis, by the way. Oh, and we're engaged. The second page is a letter I've written to Bill Cox, Sheriff of Willow Lake. It gives you permission to use my home as long as you want, and to charge things on my credit card till I get there."

"Credit card?"

He hands her one. "This is good up to ten thousand. Feel free to use it all, if you need to."

"I thought we were going together."

"We are. But just in case we get separated, or something goes wrong."

"Like what?"

"Maybe we get stopped by the police and I get detained for a few days. Maybe we have a car wreck and I have to go to the hospital. Maybe—"

"Stop. I get the point."

She folds the papers, puts them in her back pocket, and says, "This is thoughtful of you, Jack, but we're not going to be separated. From here on out, I'm sticking to you like cold spaghetti."

Chapter 23

Heading west on I-12, Jack says, "Are you sure your Emma Wilson ID is clean?"

"Far as I know."

He reaches in his jacket, hands it to her. She puts it in her jeans' pocket.

"Is it stolen?" Jack says.

"Sort of."

"What do you mean?"

"The real Emma Wilson would be my age if she were still alive, but she died in a car wreck on her ninth birthday."

"She never paid taxes?"

"Nope."

"Shit. And the only work history's the Pancake House?"

"That's the downside."

Jack frowns. "If there's an upside, I hope you'll share it with me."

"No one in Willow Lake will have any reason to check my ID too closely."

"Why's that?"

"Because we'll be a couple. And they already know *you*."

"You make it sound like you're actually going to give us a try."

"I said I would, and meant it."

A car comes roaring up behind them, draws even, and honks.

"What now?" Jack says.

"He's pointing to our trunk."

"What about it?"

"I don't know. Let's pull over and check it out."

Jack waves a thank you to the car, slows down, pulls over.

Jill jumps out, yells, "*Damn* it!" Then climbs back in the car and says, "We've got to get off the interstate, and quick."

"Why?"

"The Fosters kicked both our tail lights out!"

"Shit!"

Jack takes the next exit, turns south.

"What're you *doing*?" Jill says.

"There's bound to be a right turn soon. It'll take us straight to Baton Rouge."

"I'm *from* here, remember?"

"So?"

"There *is* no right turn. Not till you get to French Settlement. We're going *way* off course. They'll have that trunk kicked open before you know it."

"All the more reason not to go back to the interstate. What's near here?"

"Nothing but swamps."

"You sure about that?"

"Yes, of course!"

"Then what the hell is that?" Jack says, pointing straight ahead.

Chapter 24

The night sky before them is suddenly alive with flames.

"Turn around, Jack! Now!"

He slams the brake pedal, cuts the tires left, gets halfway across the road. He backs up, throws the car in drive, attempts to complete the turn, but that's as far as he gets.

Hundreds of men, women, and children converge on the road.

"What the *fuck?*"

"We're trapped!"

They appear from the marsh instantaneously, like a scene from *Walking Dead*.

Except that these people are very much alive.

A dozen men jump on the car like monkeys in a zoo riot. After posing and flexing their muscles, they take up positions on the hood, roof, and trunk of the car...

...And start dancing.

The others chant: "Soybeans! Yams! Cotton! Crabs!"

"Oh, shit!" Jill says.

"What?"

"It's the Virgin Boat Festival."

"You're making that up."

"We're going to be here a while."

"Where'd they all come from? The road was deserted a minute ago."

"It's part of the festival. There are a thousand people between here and the bayou. We hit it at the exact wrong time. This totally sucks."

"We can't even open the doors!" Jack says.

"We'll have to wait till they flame the pirogue."

"I'm sure that sentence makes perfect sense to the locals."

"These aren't locals. They're Vikings."

"Vikings?"

"It's insane. The whole stupid thing's insane. And we're stuck in the middle of it."

"For how long?"

"What time is it now?"

"Twelve-fifteen."

"It ends at dawn."

"You're shitting me."

The crowd continues to swarm. Dozens of kids tap every part of the car they can reach, while continuing their chant.

"What are they *talking* about?" Jack says.

Jill shakes her head in disgust. "Crazy, stupid, fucking festival," she says.

"Explain it to me."

"*What?* Why?"

"What else can we do? On the bright side, the Fosters aren't getting out of the trunk anytime soon. Not with all these guys dancing on it."

She smiles in spite of her anger. "They're probably wondering what the hell's going on."

"I am, too. So tell me."

"It's so *stupid!*" she says. "You'd literally think less of me if I explain it. You'll wonder how I know about something so ridiculous."

"Try me."

She sighs. "I just want to get out of here. I want to go to Willow Lake, to your lake house. Why the *fuck* did you turn south, Jack? What made you *do* that?"

When he fails to answer, she looks at him and says, "I'm sorry. I'm just so..."

"I know."

"I thought we were actually going to make it, you know?"

"We'll still get there."

"*How?* The whole world's against us!"

"You're just saying that because fifty people are licking our windows simultaneously."

It's true. Those who aren't dancing and chanting are tapping and licking.

"This is the creepiest thing I've ever seen," she says.

"Explain it to me."

"It has something to do with Vikings and their swamp relatives. They come from all over the world, show up by the thousands every twelve years."

"This only happens eight times a century?"

"That's right. And only in this one place."

"And we just happened to hit it?"

"Lucky us, right?"

"I want to hear it all, okay?"

"Okay."

"But I mainly want to know two things. Are we in danger? And where the hell were they hiding?"

"We're not in any danger. I mean, sure, they *seem* deranged. But their kids are here, and gumbo's being cooked."

"Speaking of the kids..."

"Yeah?"

"I thought Vikings were Scandinavian. You know, blond hair, blue eyes? These kids are like *Children of the Corn*."

"Except creepier."

"I don't understand why the women and kids are licking our windows. They're full of dead bugs."

"Told you they were hungry."

"When's dinner?"

"After the chant."

"How long does the chant last?"

"How the fuck should *I* know? I can only tell you what makes them stop."

"What's that?"

"Do you really give a shit?"

"I do."

She says, "I can't believe I'm saying this out loud. Okay, so they stop chanting to smoke the Jester. After that, the torch people come to light the way."

"The way to what?"

"The bayou."

"What happens there?"

"Food, drink, more singing, dancing, chanting, tapping, and licking. Not the car, but sugarcane."

"Sugarcane?"

"Then the virgins ride up on horseback, the Ging Master launches the pirogue into the bayou, and every sixth man spits on the foot of the fifth, and hurls his torch at the boat."

"Then what?"

"You're letting Ging Master slide?"

Jack shrugs.

Jill says, "Then they watch the pirogue burn in the water, down to the last ember."

"Then what?"

"Then they lie down and go to sleep."

"Back up to the part about the virgins."

She shakes her head. "Typical male response."

"Well, it's the name of the festival, after all. The Virgin Boat Festival, right? Isn't that what you said?"

She sighs. "Okay. Look. I don't know the whole story, but here's how it works. The festival starts at sundown, when all these numbskulls gather, and six topless women ride down the trail on horseback."

"Virgins?"

"They *symbolize* virgins."

"Right. Then what happens?"

"They ride down the trail till they find someone holding a chicken, and ask if they can have it for the community gumbo pot. The person answers, 'You can have what you can catch.' At that point, a bunch of live chickens are set free in a muddy, slippery, fenced-in area, and the topless women have to run around and catch enough chickens to feed the crowd, but at least six. Which is harder than it sounds. Of course, it's a crowd-pleaser, as you can imagine. When the chickens are caught, they're killed, cut up, and tossed into the community gumbo pot. While the maidens chase the chickens, the Pot Tenders chop vegetables and sausages, and get the gumbo started. They simmer it all night."

"So it's a big feast."

"That's right."

"And the chanting?"

"They're giving thanks to the food that sustains the bayou-dwellers."

"I don't understand the Viking part."

"Me either."

"What about the jester?"

"Some guy shows up dressed like a court jester, and some others build a brush fire and fan the smoke around him. He says the final chant, and lights a torch. Then a thousand people over there—" she points out the passenger window, then says, "Well, you can't see, but the bayou's a quarter mile across the marsh, in that general direction. Anyway, the bayou people light their torches and make a lighted path for all these idiots who have surrounded our car."

"So they just wait around here till a car shows up?"

"How the fuck should *I* know?"

"You seem to know a lot about this festival."

"I think our car showing up was a coincidence. They probably think we're part of the program."

"And you know all this, how?"

"There was something about it on TV, where the festival was being protested by a group of *sane* people. So anyway, this bunch joins that bunch at the bayou and they eat the gumbo and whatever other shit they've cooked all night, and drink sugarcane rum, and wait for the six maidens to lead the Pirogue Procession."

"So where was everyone hiding before the flares started firing?"

"This bunch has to lie in the marsh, quietly, in the dark, till the flares are fired. Then they jump up and start this ridiculous dance thing. It's called *The Swarming*, I think, and it has something to do with bees."

"And the licking?"

"I have no idea. And don't ask me anything else, because I've told you all I'm going to say."

"You're right," Jack says.

"About what?"

"It *is* stupid."

The chanting stops.

"*Finally!*" she says.

"What now?" Jack says.

"Showtime."

Chapter 25

The dancers and lickers quietly withdraw and the men form a wide circle around the car. With the women and children sitting on the ground in front of them, the men assume a crouching, wide-legged, fighting stance. Each warrior locks elbows with the man on either side of him.

"Oh, shit!" Jill says.

"Now what?"

"I forgot about the Circle of Hell."

"The what?"

"No one gets in, no one gets out. Except the Jester and maidens. And we're stuck in the middle."

"I thought we'd have a chance to get away when the Jester showed up," Jack says.

"Really? The way our luck's been going tonight?"

"Hey, my luck hasn't been so bad."

She looks at him incredulously.

He shrugs. "I got laid, didn't I?"

Jill frowns. "You got beat up by four different people, three of whom are still in the trunk. You killed four hunters who planned to rape you. You blew up my car. A policeman was shot. We're running for our lives because my husband wants to kill us, but you made a wrong turn that put us in the middle of the most insane festival known to man. We're trapped here, in the Circle of Hell, and policemen are coming, and—"

"What do you mean, 'policemen are coming?'"

"They invite county police to the dinner and boat launch part."

"Why?"

"To prove they're not actually sacrificing virgins."

"You're telling me the police will be here any minute?"

"If they're not here already."

It's hard to see out of the bug-smeared, saliva-soaked windows, but everyone's attention seems fixed on some torches approaching from the east. In the trunk, the Fosters pick this moment to start kicking and screaming.

"We've got to get out of here," Jack says.

He turns the windshield wipers on, presses the button to spray the wiper fluid. It takes a few seconds, but the fluid affords them a small field of vision amid the streaks and smears.

"If only we'd stolen a Dodge," Jack says.

"Why?"

"So I could say let's get the Dodge out of hell!"

"Yes, but why would you?"

"Don't you get it? Instead of saying 'let's get the hell out of Dodge?'"

She groans. "I got it the first time."

Jack says, "I thought you were the one who likes word-play."

"Jack."

"What?"

"If you've got a plan, execute it now. Because the women and children are coming over to check our trunk."

"No time to see the topless ladies?"

"They're only topless for the chicken chase."

"And that already happened?"

"Hours ago."

"In that case, brace yourself!"

Jack presses the horn, throws the car in gear, and peels out. The Vikings are wide-eyed, but hold their positions, daring him to run them down. The women and children are less daring.

They scatter.

Jack speeds up.

As the car closes in on the men blocking their way, Jack says, "I'm not going to stop."

"You can't just kill them."

"It's their job to move."

The Vikings agree. At the last moment, they jump out of the way, and the Oldsmobile barrels down the highway.

"*Oh my God, Jack!*" she shouts. "That was *amazing!*"

"Circle of Hell, my ass!" he says.

"Keep going straight," Jill says, as they approach the interstate.

He passes the on-ramp, goes under the interstate, and passes four dirt roads before spying a road block in the distance.

"Shit!" Jack says.

"What now?"

He points up ahead.

"You think they're looking for us?"

"Probably not, but the way our luck's been running—"

"I agree," Jill says. "What now?"

"We head back. Take one of the dirt roads we passed."

"Which one?"

"Does it matter?"

"No. They all lead to boat ramps, eventually."

"Are you certain?"

"No, but it makes sense. This area is all bayous and fishing camps."

"Maybe we can find one and hole up."

"Hole up? What are you, a gangster from the thirties?"

Jack passes the first dirt road.

"What's wrong with that one?"

"I've got an idea."

"What?"

"Well, it's more of a contingency plan."

He passes two more dirt roads, comes to the last one before the interstate, and turns right.

"Slow down," Jill says.

"Why?"

"You'll kick up less dust."

"Good point."

He gets about a quarter-mile down the road before the Fosters start kicking and screaming again.

Jack says, "Any idea what to do about the Fosters?"

"Nothing comes to mind."

A mile later the road dead-ends. Jack and Jill roll their windows down and look for signs of life.

"Where's the boat ramp you were talking about?" Jack says. "I only see two empty fishing shacks."

"Guess I was wrong about that," she says.

"There's bound to be a bayou nearby, though."

"Of course. And it'll be filled with snakes, alligators, and spiders. Please tell me your plan doesn't include stealing a boat."

"I wouldn't know where to take it," Jack says. "I'm a city guy. Rowing through the Louisiana swamps in the wee hours of the morning strikes me as a bad plan. We could get lost pretty quick. I was hoping to find another car to steal. Or someone we could pay to drive us."

Jack backs up a hundred yards, turns the car around, heads toward the main road.

"What now?" Jill says.

"Plan B."

He parks the car a quarter-mile from the main road, turns the engine off, removes the key. Then opens the door, gets out.

Jill climbs out the passenger side.

"What are we doing?"

"Is there anything you need to get from the car?"

"All I've got's the filthy clothes I'm wearing."

"Need to use the bathroom?"

"No."

"Me either. Let's go."

"Where?"

"I don't want to say out loud."

Jack opens the trunk, and the Fosters cower, thinking they're about to be shot.

"You're okay," he says. "Sorry about the dents all over your car. We're heading out now, but I'll leave the trunk open. Eventually you'll be able to work yourselves free. If you keep quiet, I'll leave your car keys at the end of the dirt road."

"What if we scream and holler?" the old lady says.

"I'll keep the keys."

With that, Jack and Jill start walking toward the main road. When they get out of hearing distance, Jill says, "What's the plan? Hitchhike?"

"I don't like our chances of getting picked up this time of night. I think we should go back to the festival and try to blend in. Maybe meet someone there, pay them to give us a ride after the boat-burning."

"You just want some gumbo."

"That too. But I think some of the Vikings will go home after the boat-burning. Wouldn't you?"

"Instead of sleeping on a blanket in the mosquito and snake-infested marsh? I certainly would. Then again, I wouldn't be out here in the first place."

Jack says, "We should re-think your Baton Rouge plan."

"Why?"

"I like the idea of catching a cab to Memphis, then changing cabs. But we've already lost a lot of time. If we're going to pay someone to drive us we should go to Jackson. It'll save us two hours of driving time."

When they get to the main road, Jack stops, takes a knee, places the car keys on the ground, and grabs a handful of dirt.

"What're you doing now?"

"Getting my game face on."

He rubs some dirt on his face, then hers. Then they begin the two-mile walk they hope will end with a bowl of gumbo and a ride to Jackson, Mississippi.

"Think we'll get fed?" he says.

"That would make a perfect day for you, wouldn't it? Four fights, some pussy, and a bowl of gumbo."

Chapter 26

By the time they infiltrate the Viking throng, Jack and Jill are thoroughly exhausted.

It's been an especially long night for Jill.

She's been drugged, kidnapped, bound, and stuck in a car for hours. She's been shot at, made love to, forced to assault a teenager, and two septuagenarians. She's been threatened by not only a bounty hunter, but also a state trooper, a jilted husband, and a quartet of bisexual redneck deer hunters. She's not only a witness to a quadruple homicide and cop-shooting, she's also committed breaking-and-entering, three counts of assault with a deadly weapon, three counts of kidnapping, and a car-jacking. She's currently on the run with her husband's employee, and has reason to believe she's being hunted by the state police and her vengeful husband. She hasn't slept in twenty hours, hasn't had anything to eat since breakfast yesterday, and precious little to drink. As they approach the torch-lit tables, she reminds herself the key here is to blend in, get some gumbo, something to drink, and lay low.

There are half as many revelers as she expected. A thousand at most, she guesses, and maybe a half-dozen policemen, who may or may not be on Bobby's payroll. She's worried about being recognized. Not by the cops, but...

"*Princess!*" a lady shouts.

Jill turns her head, tries to move away.

Jack says, "Is she talking to *you?*"

"Princess! I lay at your feet!" the lady yells.

"Jack! Get me out of here!" Jill says.

Before he can react, the lady jumps on top of the table where Jack and Jill are sitting with a dozen revelers.

"What the hell?" Jack says.

The woman is Jill's age, but her head is completely bald, and painted bright red. When she's not speaking, her tongues flick out from her mouth like a snake's. In truth, she has but one tongue, but it's been split in the center all the way to the back of her throat.

There's something else unusual about her tongue: it's bright blue.

"Princess!" she says. "It's me, Princess Lillith!"

"Shhh!" Jill says.

Lillith crows like a rooster and yells, "Chieftans, noblemen, freemen, wives, maidens, lords-in-training: I give you Princess Thyra!"

Those at the table, and within hearing distance, gasp, and fall to their knees.

Jill whispers, "Please, Fanny. I'm trying to keep a low profile."

"Seriously?"

"Yes."

Fanny shouts, "My mistake! A thousand apologies to you all. Please, resume your revelry!"

The group murmurs and mumbles, and she climbs down from the table and whispers, "Whatever you need, Jill. Meet me at the fires."

She looks at Jack and says, "Hi, handsome." To Jill she says, "How long have you been hitting that?"

"We'll meet you at the fires," Jill says.

Jack says, "Are you one of the virgin riders?"

Her forked, blue tongue slides out of her mouth. "You got a problem with that?"

"Nope. I'm just sorry I missed the chicken chase."

"Why, because you wanted to see these?"

She lowers her tunic, exposes her breasts.

Several men at the table start clapping. Fanny bows.

Jill says, "What are you *doing*, Fanny?"

"Being lusty. Like mom always said, nothing says howdie like flashing your tits."

"Your mom sounds like a wise lady," Jack says.

She pulls her tunic back up and says, "I'm Fanny. Who are you?"

"Jack."

"Nice to meet you. Just so you know, I'm available, in case this thing with Jill doesn't work out."

"Good to know," he says, winking at Jill.

Jill frowns. "Let's walk to the fires and talk."

Jack wolfs down the rest of his gumbo, then he and Jill follow Fanny to one of the fire pits.

Jill says, "We need a ride to Jackson, Mississippi."

"I'd love to help you, hon, but I'm on the back of a Harley, Nashville bound."

"I thought you lived in Minnesota."

"That was years ago. I've got a private dick gig now."

"That sounds lusty," Jack says.

"It means I'm working with a private investigator."

"Where?"

"You remember Dani Ripper? The Little Girl Who Got Away?"

"Who doesn't? She was all over the news. They found her, right?"

"She found herself. Resurfaced when her husband was murdered."

"You're a private investigator?" Jill says.

"No. I'm her receptionist."

Jack says, "She's okay about the...uh..."

"The what?"

"Well, no offense, but your head's painted red, and you've got a blue, forked tongue."

Fanny says, "Dani hasn't actually met me yet."

"How'd you get the job?"

"Enough about me. How'd you get here, hitchhike?" She frowns. "You're not broke, are you, handsome?"

"No. But our car's been disabled."

"Wait! Was that *you* a while ago? In the Circle of Hell?"

"*Shh!*" Jill whispers. "Keep your voice down."

Fanny whispers, "What was going on in the trunk?"

"It's a long story."

Fanny says, "I can find you a ride, but you'll need more cash than I've got on me. I can spot you fifty. Maybe we could take up a collection."

"How much would we need?"

"About two hundred."

Jack says, "Two hundred bucks for a ride to Jackson?"

"That's right, handsome. But if it was me taking you, I'd work it out in trade."

"I've got enough cash," he says. "But we need to leave right now."

"For right now it's two grand."

"*What?*"

"I'm assuming the law's involved?"

"Not necessarily."

"I can get you to Jackson in an hour. But these revelers won't take you."

"Why not?"

"They came from all over the world to be here. They're not going to leave till it's over."

"Then how can you possibly get us to Jackson in an hour? It took me longer than that to drive here tonight."

"You won't be driving."

Jill says, "What have you got in mind?"

"Ever see the movie, *Planes, Trains and Automobiles?*"

Jack says, "What about it?"

"This will be like that. Only different."

"What's that supposed to mean?"

"You'll see."

Chapter 27

Jack starts to count out some money.

Fanny says, "Not here."

"Why? We're completely alone."

"It's too dark. You could be giving me newsprint, for all I know."

Jill digs an angry elbow into Jack's ribs and says, "Newsprint?"

Fanny says, "Pretty boys like Jack can be really dumb when it comes to women. They'll do anything to get in my pants."

"I have no interest in what's inside your pants!" Jack says.

"And that's what proves you're dumb," Fanny says.

Jill laughs.

Fanny leads them to a hard-packed mud alley between two giant tents with generator-powered lights. Ten feet away, on either side, the tents are bustling with people and activity. They're enclosed, and the fabric throws off enough light for them to see each other clearly.

Fanny holds her hand out, Jack places ten bills in it.

"What's this?" she says.

"Half up front."

"Which one of you is staying behind?"

"Neither. This is a deposit. Fifty percent down. That's how I do business."

"You know how I do business?" she says.

"How's that?"

"If you give me half the money to buy a dog, I'll sell you half a dog."

Jill says, "It's okay, Jack. Fanny won't cheat us."

He frowns, hands Fanny another thousand.

She shocks him by kissing him flush on the mouth. He tries to back up, but she grabs his shirt to hold him in place. Ignoring the look of disgust on his face, Fanny works her cleaved tongue past his lips, and tries to breach the barricade he's created with his teeth.

"Fanny?" Jill says.

She backs off reluctantly, flicks her tongue out.

Jack grimaces. Says, "Why'd you *do* that?"

"I was letting you thank me for helping you."

Jill silently counts to ten, attempting to keep her temper in check.

"Wait here," Fanny says. "I'll be right back."

When she disappears into the night, Jill says, "What was that all about?"

"Which part?"

"The part where you talked her into flashing her boobs, and tongue-kissed her."

He prepares to launch an argument to set the record straight, but stops himself.

"You're changing the subject," he says.

"What subject?"

"An hour ago you told me all about this stupid festival, but you left out two things: Princess Thyra, and how you became friends with Fanny."

"Twelve years ago I was one of the six maidens."

"You were eighteen then?"

"Yes."

"Naked, on a horse?"

"Topless. Not naked."

"How many chickens did you catch?"

"Fuck you."

"No, really."

"Two."

"Wish I could have seen that."

"Me, too. You might have saved me a miserable decade."

They kiss.

"How'd you meet Fanny?"

"Fuck you, Jack!"

"What now?"

"You kiss me and the first words out of your mouth are about Fanny?"

"My first words were about you. I asked how *you* met Fanny."

"Sounds like a technicality to me."

"Fine. Don't tell me. I'm just glad your head and tongue are normal."

"She was one of the maidens last time out."

"You guys are Vikings?"

"No. We were campaign volunteers. The governor's re-election committee paid us a thousand dollars to be maidens."

"I'd have paid twice that much to see you topless, chasing chickens!"

"Thanks. I think."

They kiss again. From behind them, Fanny says, "Get a room!"

Jack and Jill turn to see Fanny sitting on a horse, holding the reigns of a second one.

"Two horses for three people?" Jack says.

"I've got to bring them back," she says. "I can't lead two horses by myself through this crowd. Jill, I'll let you choose who gets to sit behind me on the saddle."

"Me," Jill says.

"Sorry, Jack," Fanny says. "Okay, let's saddle up."

They climb on the horses, work their way through the crowd, through the marsh, and onto the main road. They ride under the interstate, and come to the dirt road where Jack and Jill left the Fosters. Jack stands in his stirrups to see if the car's still there, but it's too dark to tell.

"Fanny, hold up," he says. "I need to check something."

He climbs off his horse, hands her the reigns, and checks to see if the keys are still where he put them.

When he reclaims his horse, Jill says, "Update?"

"The Fosters have left the building."

"Who are the Fosters?" Fanny says.

"The less you know, the better," Jack says.

"Story of my life."

"Story of *my* life is paying two thousand dollars to ride a horse back to where I was an hour ago."

They ride to the next dirt road and turn left. After a half mile it ends at an old, two-story bait shop. Fanny ties the horses to a cypress tree, and knocks on the door till the lights come on upstairs. The window opens, a man yells, "We're closed!"

"Ziggy, open up. It's me, Fanny."

"*Fanny?* Where the hell have you *been*, girl?"

"Everywhere. Open up, I've got some paying customers for you."

"Hang on."

Fanny whispers, "I'll go in first, and handle the negotiations. Don't say anything about the money you've paid or how much you have in your pockets."

Ziggy opens the door, Fanny walks in, closes the door behind her.

Jack says, "What's going on, you think?"

"Fanny's resourceful," Jill says.

"What's that mean?"

"She's planning to pay him with sex and pocket the difference. Or at least part of it."

"She told you that while riding here?"

"That and a whole lot more, including detailed information about the tattoos on her ass, all of which comes under the heading of too much information."

"Did she happen to mention how we were getting to Jackson within an hour?"

"Ziggy's going to air boat us to a private airfield. Then we're flying to another private airfield in Jackson. From there, we can take a cab to Memphis, then another one to Willow Lake."

"Ziggy doesn't have a car or truck?"

"Nope."

"I don't want our names appearing on an FAA flight manifest."

"They won't."

"Why not?"

"We're being flown by a drug runner. In a crop duster."

"Oh, swell!"

The door opens. Fanny says, "Let's go."

"You're going with us?" Jill says.

"I'll want to pay Mike the Pilot personally. Otherwise, Ziggy might be inclined to shoot you in the back, dump you in the swamp, and steal your money."

"What stops him from killing all three of us?"

She flicks her blue tongue and says, "He'll want me in a happy mood."

Chapter 28

"How fast will she go?" Jack says, as they climb aboard.

"This one can carry two passengers at seventy-eight miles an hour," Ziggy says. "We'll probably hit fifty on the way there. But coming back I plan to open her up."

"The boat or me?" Fanny says.

"Both."

Jill says, "You're not seriously planning to go fifty miles an hour in the dark, are you?"

"Did you bring a spotlight?"

"No."

"Then yes, I am."

"That seems *terribly* dangerous."

"It is, for a fact," Ziggy says.

They travel nine miles in twelve terrifying minutes. All four of them scream the entire way, including Ziggy, who screams the loudest. Jack and Jill can't get off the boat fast enough. Fanny says, "I can't wait to take her seventy-eight in pitch black, after the sissies are gone."

"I'm game," Ziggy says, "But I'll need another drink first."

They hear him unscrew the cap from his bourbon flask.

"Drink till it hurts!" Fanny says.

"Hurry back, Sugar Tits."

She leads Jack and Jill to the grass runway where they find Mike the Pilot standing beside the plane. "One thousand," he says. "In advance."

Fanny pays him and says, "Who's first?"

Jill says, "What do you mean?"

"It's a crop-duster. Mike can only carry one passenger at a time."

Jack says, "You didn't say anything about that."

"If I did, you might not have come."

"That's my point."

"But here we are," Fanny says. "Look, it's only a forty minute flight. I called a cab before we left Ziggy's place. He'll be there when you land. Mike will fly one of you there, come back and get the other one in ninety minutes."

The only light comes from two battery-powered lanterns on either side of the runway. Jack and Jill can see each other, but their faces are shadowy.

Jack says, "You go first. You can't stay here by yourself. It's too dangerous."

Jill says, "I don't want to go without you."

"Guys," Jack says, "Can you give us a minute to talk? We'll be right back."

He and Jill walk far enough to insure privacy.

Jack says, "I'm sure everything will be fine. But just in case, here."

He hands her the cash envelope and says, "I kept five hundred, in case Mike needs an extra incentive at the last minute."

"I don't want to carry all this money."

"These guys don't know if I've got any money, or if so, how much. But I doubt they'll think you're holding it. If they decide to rob me at the last minute, we'll both be without cash."

"Fine. I'll hold it till you get there. But I don't want to split up."

"I know."

"What if he tries something when we land?"

"Like what?"

"Like...you know."

"Fanny says she called a cab. You trust her, right?"

"Completely."

"Okay then, when you land, go straight to the cab."

"What if something goes wrong?"

He sighs. "We're sort of locked in at this point, Jill. But I want you to promise me something. If I'm not there two hours after you land, go without me."

"I can't."

"You have to."

"If you're not there in two hours it'll mean you're dead."

"Probably. But it also might mean the plane broke down. Or some other issue came up."

"Like what?"

"I don't know. I'm just saying, do *not* wait more than two hours for me."

They watch Mike the pilot illuminate two lanterns at the far end of the airstrip.

Jack says, "Look, I've still got my cell phone, and you've got my number in your pocket. When you land, get the cab driver to call me, so I'll know you're safe."

"What if you don't answer?"

"If you can't reach me on my cell phone, or if I take off and don't arrive on schedule, do *not* wait. If I'm alive, I'll find a way to get to you."

"Don't ditch me, Jack."

He laughs. "If I were ditching you I wouldn't give you my cash, my credit card, and my lake house keys, would I?"

Mike hollers, "Turn on those other two lamps for me, and let's get going!"

Jack says, "Walk with me."

As they head to the far end of the runway, Jill says, "Technically, you haven't given me your lake house keys."

"I can't. I lost them in the car fire. But when you get to the house, look for the water spigot on the left side of the house. It's been taped. Unravel the tape, and you'll find the extra key."

"You sound like you're not coming."

"I'm just trying to protect you in case something goes wrong. If I'm alive, I'll meet you there, eventually. I promise."

They turn on the lanterns.

"What if something happens to *me*?" Jill says.

"When you get to Willow Lake, stock up on provisions. You'll want to buy some clothes and a disposable cell phone.

When you get a chance, get a stepladder. You can keep it in the hall closet."

"Why a stepladder?"

"Any messages you want to give me, like your new cell phone number, or anything else you want to tell me, you can write on the top edge of the doors. No one will ever think to look for them there."

Mike fires up the plane.

Fanny shouts, "We're sittin' on G, waitin' on O!"

"She'll be right there!" Jack shouts back.

To Jill, he says, "One last thing."

"What?"

"I need to tell you about my secret room."

Chapter 29

Fifty-two minutes later, Jack's cell phone rings.

"Thank God you answered!" Jill says. "I've been scared to death for you. Is everything okay?"

"Everything's fine."

"Tell me Fanny's not with you."

"You mean Sugar Tits? She and Ziggy roared out of here before you were in the air. Where's Mike?"

"He took off a few minutes ago."

"Good. And the cab driver's okay?"

"Seems fine."

"I should hang up now, save the battery."

"Okay, but do me a favor?"

"Name it."

"Call me before you take off."

"Of course."

Fifty minutes later Jack places the call. The cab driver answers by giving his name, then passes the phone to Jill.

Jack says, "I'm climbing in now. I'll see you in forty-five minutes."

"What time is it now?"

"Two forty-five."

"Be safe."

"See you soon, pretty lady."

"Please hurry!"

Part Three:
A BEER AND A SANDWICH

Chapter 1

Jack climbs in the crop duster's passenger seat. "Thanks for accommodating me."

"Thanks for the extra five hundred."

They take off without speaking. When they're airborne, Jack says, "I can't believe you can land this thing in pitch dark with just six lanterns to guide you."

Mike laughs. "Six lamps is a luxury!"

Fifteen minutes into the flight Jack notices they're losing altitude rapidly.

"Anything wrong?" he says.

"I need to make a quick stop."

"For what?"

"Cargo."

"I thought we had an understanding."

"We do. But I'm in a jam."

"What do you mean?"

"After dropping your lady friend off, my boss called and asked me to pick up a shipment. It would have taken me an hour to go there and come back to get you, but you wanted to take off immediately, and offered to pay me the extra five, which I really appreciate. Truth is, I need the money. So I owe you. On the other hand, my boss has been known to kill those who piss him off. So I decided to take you to Jackson, and pick up my shipment on the way."

"How long will it take to load the plane?"

"Ten minutes."

"That seems awfully quick."

"My hopper holds seven hundred gallons of bug juice. Of course, I don't fill it with chemical spray."

"I'll go out on a limb and guess you smuggle weed."

"How'd you come to *that* conclusion?"

"You've got a crop duster you don't use for spraying crops. You fly by night. Take off and land by lamplight on private runways. And your boss kills people."

Mike laughs. "You're trying to sound all Sherlock Holmes, but the truth is Fanny told you about the weed. I know because she admitted it when she vouched for you. How it works is the ground crew has a five hundred gallon hopper they stuff with bricks of weed. When we land, all they have to do is fit the small hopper into the big one. Ten minutes to load, ten to unload. They've got it down to a science."

Moments later they touch down on a grass runway, and coast to a stop.

Mike's right. It takes virtually no time to load the cargo.

What he failed to mention is where they were landing.

Twenty miles from La Pierre.

And who'd be there, holding a gun on Jack while the ground crew worked their magic.

Jill's husband, Bobby DiPiese.

Bobby says, "There are two words you can say here you can't say in a regular airport."

"What's that?"

"Hi Jack."

Chapter 2

"You killed all four hunters?" Bobby says, forty minutes later.

"I had the element of surprise on my side."

"Don't be humble. That's an impressive bit of killing. Unfortunately, your little pit stop cost me a fortune with Officer Hank."

They're in Bobby's den. Bobby's goons, Bronson and Doug, confiscated his phone and wallet at the airfield. Bobby's working hard to pretend nothing's wrong, but Jack knows controlled fury when he sees it. He decides to play it cool, knowing that will piss Bobby off more than begging forgiveness.

Bobby says, "You'll stay the night?"

"I wouldn't want to intrude."

"What kind of host would I be not to offer? You've gone to a lot of trouble to find my loving wife."

"In that case, I'd be honored to be your guest," Jack says.

They look at each other, aware Bobby's holding all the cards.

He says, "I understand Jill caught an earlier flight."

"She did. I assume she arrived here safely? That was the plan."

Bobby smiles. "You got balls, I'll give you that. Yeah, she arrived safely. But not here."

"No?"

Bobby says, "You ever heard of synchronicity?"

Jack says nothing.

Bobby says, "It has to do with incredible coincidences. Like in this book I read, a young doctor's driving along a Texas highway one night and witnesses a car crash. He jumps out and saves a kid's life. That single event causes the kid to study medicine and eventually become a doctor. One night he's driving the exact same stretch of Texas highway and witnesses a car crash. He jumps out and saves a man's life. Turns out to be the same doctor who saved his life twenty years earlier."

"My opinion?" Jack says. "That's a bullshit story."

Bobby shrugs. "If it didn't sound like bullshit, it wouldn't qualify as synchronicity."

"Since you're telling me this, can I assume an incredible coincidence has occurred?"

"Two, actually. The first is when you turned your phone off."

"How's that a coincidence?"

"It told me you had a change of heart. So I told my guys to put the word out to everyone in Louisiana and Mississippi who works for me. We started with off-duty cops, who set up phony roadblocks on the back roads. Then we called our truckers and pilots. Low and behold, one of our pilots got the call ten minutes after dropping Jill off at a private airfield near Jackson, Mississippi."

Jack works hard to keep his face from falling.

Bobby notices the effort, twists the knife by saying, "Jill was in a cab, waiting for someone. Any idea who?"

"Sorry. I don't know her well enough to guess."

Bobby says, "According to Mike, she was waiting for you."

"But you know better."

"To be honest, Jack, I'm leaning Mike's way on this."

"What's the second coincidence?"

"The cab driver at the Jackson airfield? The one sitting with Jill?"

"Yeah?"

"Vick Wamby. He works for me."

"Bullshit."

"Synchronicity, Jack. There are twenty-two cabbies working that county, and a hundred who could have received a call for an emergency ride. But out of all those drivers, only one's on my payroll. Vick Wamby."

"If that's true, where's Jill?"

He smiles. "You'll be pleased to know she'll be here shortly."

"How?"

"Mike went to fetch her."

"He'll never get her here."

"Why not?"

"She'll run away. Or jump out of the plane."

"I spoke to her. She's coming voluntarily."

"I don't believe it."

"And yet, it's true. I told her if she came straight here without incident, I'd let you go."

Jack pauses. "Why would she care if you let me go or not?"

"That's the same question I keep asking myself, Jack."

"I don't buy it. She hates my guts. She spent the whole night trying to get away."

Bobby goes quiet a few minutes. Then says, "Remember the word I taught you?"

"Synchronicity?"

"I have another coincidence to report."

Jack waits.

Bobby says, "Tonight, I was all worked up. I get that way sometimes."

"Who doesn't?"

"Most people, actually. Not the way I do, at least. When I get all worked up I want to beat the living shit out of someone. Literally."

"Literally?"

"That's right. Take Jill, for instance. Tonight when you called and told me you were on the way, I got all worked up. I wanted to beat her, Jack. Beat her till she pissed herself. Beat her till she moved her bowels. Beat her till she literally shit blood. But I also wanted to fuck her, you know? Because you never lose those romantic feelings. So I worked it all out in my head. I planned to beat her, fuck her, beat her some more, fuck her some more, then beat her to within an inch of her life. Then you know what I planned to do? Fuck that last inch out of her. Make my dick the murder weapon."

"That's so *romantic*," Jack says, sarcastically. "You must have been *stunned* to hear she ran away."

"What can I tell you? She's an ungrateful bitch."

"But you'll show her."

"Damn right I will. Soon as she gets here."

"When will that be?"

He looks at his watch. "An hour, maybe less. The coincidence is, I got all worked up, all ready for her, then you stiffed me. I go into my office, mad as hell, and notice a package was delivered earlier today."

He motions to Doug. "Get me that container."

A moment later, Doug returns with a glass jar.

Bobby says, "Put it on the coffee table."

Bobby and Jack stare at the jar until Bobby says, "You're here now, and Jill's on the way. Rest up, Jack. I've got plans for you, after I'm done with Jill."

"Sounds like fun."

Bobby smiles a thin-lipped smile. "Oh, it *will* be!"

"That's what counts," Jack says, though his posturing sounds hollow, even to him.

Bobby stares closely at Jack's face while saying, "I'll apologize in advance for Jill's screams."

"Quite all right," Jack says. "I've been driving all night. I'm sure I'll sleep right through it. Have fun and forget I'm here."

"We'll do that," Bobby says.

He makes a gesture, and Jack is instantly flanked by Bronson and Doug.

"I'll plan on sleeping in tomorrow," Bobby says. "If you get up before me, go to the kitchen and tell Tilly what you want. But don't leave till we have a chance to settle up."

"I'm on foot," Jack says. "You think one of your guys can drive me to the Baton Rouge airport tomorrow?"

"Like I said, you got balls, kid. For now."

He looks at the goons. "Gentlemen? Please escort Mr. Tallow to his quarters."

Jack stands, follows Bronson out the room, with Doug close behind.

Chapter 3

The shrieking starts thirty minutes after Jack enters his room.

Three screams, female voice. Then it stops.

He rushes to the door, tries to get out, but it's locked. He bangs it with his fist.

From the other side, Bronson yells, "What's up, Jack?"

"I'd like the door unlocked," Jack says.

"I'd like a bigger dick," Bronson says. "What would you like, Doug?"

"A smaller one."

"Funny," Bronson says.

Jack says, "What if there's a fire in the middle of the night?"

"We'll put it out. You should feel very secure having two guards outside your door all night."

"You're saying I'm a prisoner here? Is that how you want to play this?"

"You're our guest," Doug says. "It's our job to keep you safe till Mr. Dee says you can go."

"What if Mr. Dee tells you to *fuck* each other?"

"We'll let you watch."

"I heard screams."

"That was Mrs. Dee. I patched sound into your room. Mr. Dee wanted you to hear the beating he's giving Mrs. Dee tonight."

"Sounds like family business to me," Jack says. "I'd rather have a sandwich, maybe a glass of water. Can we visit the kitchen, let me make a snack? I haven't eaten since noon."

"You've got a well-stocked bar and refrigerator in the little hallway between the bedroom and bath. I'll put the sound on while you eat. When you're ready to sleep, knock on the door, and I'll shut the sound off."

Jack hears a small click, looks up, notices speakers in the ceiling. If his room's wired for sound, he's probably being filmed. He goes to the refrigerator, checks the contents, wonders if the food or water is spiked. He doubts it.

The scream sounded like Jill's voice, but it could've been anyone. Jack says a silent prayer that Bobby's bluffing, trying to get him to react one way or the other, as he gauges how guilty Jack is.

Which makes Jack that much more determined not to tip his hand.

As long as he can believe the scream didn't come from Jill, he'll be able to maintain his cool. Eating's the last thing on Jack's mind, but for the benefit of the cameras, assuming there are some, he grabs a sandwich and a bottle of beer, takes them to the bed, sits and eats.

Then he hears Jill begging Bobby not to hit her.

Jack's heart sinks. It's definitely Jill.

And she sounds desperate.

He throws the sandwich and beer against the wall and screams her name.

Jill shrieks, "I swear to God! There's no one else! I've been faithful!"

Bobby shouts, "You ran off! You fucking *ran off*!"

The sounds of Bobby's brutality are unmistakable. It's a sound Jack has heard all his life.

Fists hitting flesh.

Jill's sobbing. Begging. But Bobby's relentless. He hits her. Hits her again, harder. Her body slams into a wall. She cries out in pain. There are short pauses, punctuated by sharp slapping sounds, and Jill's screams.

For ten minutes it continues.

Finally, there's another sickening smack, another crash against the wall, and the crying stops.

Two minutes later, Jack hears Jill whimpering like a child.

"Please!" she says. "Please don't."

Bobby's grunting, not speaking.

Jack can't guess the details of how it's going down, but based on the sound alone, it's clear Bobby's raping her. As if he needs further clarification, he hears Bronson and Doug cheering.

Bronson yells, "Give it to her, Mr. Dee!"

Doug hollers, "Take it, bitch! Take it all!"

Bronson says, "You hear that? That's anal! I guarantee you, he's giving her anal! God, I wish it was me!"

"You wish Mr. Dee would give you anal?" Doug says.

"Funny," Bronson says.

"I think so," Doug says. "But I wonder if Jack does."

The grunting continues. Between each grunt, Jack can hear Jill's cries of pain.

Tomorrow I'm going to kill them, Jack says to himself. *I'm going to kill them all.*

Chapter 4

"Jack, you look *terrible!*" Bobby says, with a mocking tone. "Did you not sleep at *all?*"

It's ten a.m. They're sitting at Bobby's kitchen table. Tilly the cook has prepared an assortment of food for their breakfast. Under different circumstances, Jack would be all over the biscuits and sausage gravy.

Bobby's kitchen has three doorways. One leads to the dining room, one to the butler's pantry and bar area. The third leads to a hallway with a bathroom, laundry room, and an exit. Three goons are guarding the doorways, and none of them are Doug and Bronson.

Bobby's right. Jack didn't sleep last night, didn't even attempt it. Jill's beating was horrific, endless, and featured distinct rounds, like a boxing match. Round one? Verbal abuse. Round two? Physical assault. Round three? Sexual assault. Round four? A quiet period, where the sound was turned off. Rounds five through eight? Repeat. Rounds nine through twelve? Repeat.

Bad as the beatings were, and the sexual assaults, the quiet times were even worse. When the sound went dead, he prayed to hear her scream again, knowing that even though she was in pain, at least she was still alive.

As long as Jill was alive, there was hope.

But that was then, and this is now, and Bobby's gloating.

Jack's face is impassive, but only one thing is preventing him from leaping across the table and strangling his host to death.

He's tied to his chair.

A rope binds his feet and ankles to the chair legs. Another rope binds his lap to the seat. Another binds his stomach and chest to the chair back. Another binds his right hand to the chair arm. Only his left hand remains unbound, so he can eat.

The idea being, if he decides to throw something at Bobby, his left hand won't be as accurate. Of course, Bobby's hedged the bet by removing all metal utensils, the salt and pepper shakers, the gravy bowl, and the china from Jack's limited field of reach. If Jack's going to throw something, his options are limited to a plastic fork, a paper plate, and whatever food he can grab.

"I didn't get much sleep either," Bobby says, holding his hands up so Jack can see they've been taped. He adds, "It's not as easy as you think, beating a defenseless woman all night. Really bruises the fists and hands."

"I know she fought back," Jack says.

"Sorry to disappoint you, sport, but she wasn't as feisty as you'd like to think. She cried, begged, and accepted most of the beating in a fetal position. Of course, I stretched her out time and again, to inflict the maximum pain possible. I pounded every inch of her body with my fists."

"You're a sick bastard. I wish I'd killed her yesterday, to spare her the pain and humiliation."

"I don't blame you for feeling guilty, Jack. You let her down, no doubt about it."

Bobby puts some biscuits on his plate, splits them in half, ladles gravy over them, grabs some bacon, fried potatoes, and onions.

"You should eat," he says. "Want me to call Tilly in? Have her prepare a plate of food for you?"

"I don't eat with psychopaths."

Bobby laughs. "You're upset with me."

"Fuck you."

"You were on camera last night, during the beating. I was preoccupied, of course, but my guys pulled clips for me to watch this morning. I couldn't help but notice you appeared to be distressed whenever Jill cried out in pain."

"Any normal human being would have the same reaction."

"Maybe. But I think there's another reason."

Jack looks at Bobby through venomous eyes.

Bobby says, "If you'll remember, there were long periods of time where you heard nothing. That was me, turning off the microphone. I didn't want you to hear the interrogation, or Jill's confession. I wanted to give you a chance to confess every last detail, and see if your stories matched. Before I ask you what happened, I'll say two things. First, Jill told me everything. Second, to her credit, it took a long time to get it out of her."

Jack lowers his head, squeezes his eyes shut.

"You know what I think?" Bobby says.

"I don't give a shit."

He nibbles a piece of bacon and says, "Crazy as it sounds, I think she actually believed you were going to save her, somehow."

Jack looks up at him.

"That hope, that belief in you, kept her going. No matter what I did to her, she denied everything. Denied you two had a connection. Denied you were running off together. She even denied you had *sex*! And frankly, I gave up. Beating and fucking her like that? For all those hours? I gotta tell you, that took a lot out of me."

He sighs, waves a hand, dismissively. "Maybe it's because I'm old. Maybe it's because it was so late when we started. But the truth is I couldn't get it out of her."

Jack's face lights up. "She's still *alive*?"

"What I'm saying, I couldn't get her to confess by beating her. *You* got her to confess, though. Without saying a word."

"What the *fuck* are you talking about?"

"Remember when Jill began screaming? I'm talking about the very first screams. Three in a row, if I remember correctly. I don't want to say what I did to make her do that. But there's a digital counter on the tape that shows you in the guest room, listening to her. I showed that clip to Jill. Her screams, the tape count. A few minutes later, more screams. Her, getting beat up, begging for her life, you, sitting on the bed, eating a sandwich, drinking a beer..."

He pauses, then says, "You broke her heart, Jack."

Jack stares at him blankly. What he's saying, the whole macho act he put on for Bobby's sake backfired. And wasn't it Jill who told him to be himself, and stop acting so tough all the time? Didn't she, in fact, tell him not to underestimate Bobby?

Bobby says, "Seeing you calmly eat a sandwich while she begged for her life took all the fight out of her. She confessed everything, voluntarily. Said she'd been a fool to believe in you. And that's when I saw it."

He spears a piece of potato, eats it, and says, "I looked in her eyes and everything was different. Like someone turned out the lights. And that's when I realized she was within an inch of dying. So I bravely climbed on top of her and did what I said I'd do. I fucked that last inch of life out of her."

He laughs, finishes his breakfast, then says, "All night long I punished that woman, trying to make her apologize for running away. But she never did. I couldn't understand it. I mean, if someone's beating the shit out of you, and you knew they wanted an apology, wouldn't you say you're sorry?"

He shakes his head and goes quiet. Eventually, he says, "It took a long time, but it finally dawned on me. You know what I'm going to say, don't you?"

Jack says nothing.

Bobby says, "She was taking that beating for *you*. So naturally, I tried to get her to confess she'd had sex with you. Tried to make her admit you were planning to run away together. She wouldn't, so I beat her harder. Beat her till my hands hurt. Beat the nipples off her tits. At that point I didn't even care about her running away, all I wanted was her confession. And no matter what I did, she denied it. It's like she knew she had that one power over me, and she held on to it like a Senator clutches a bribe. And you know what? The bitch won. She beat me. Like *Cool Hand Luke*, she won the fight by never quitting...until she saw the video of you in the guest room. When she saw that, I didn't even have to ask. She spilled her guts. Told me everything."

He laughs again. "All it took was a beer and a sandwich."

Chapter 5

Jack sits there quietly, tears filling his eyes.

"If I were a member of a jury," Bobby says, "I'd take those tears as a sign of your guilt."

"Keep that in mind, you pompous bastard. When *you* go to court."

Bobby chuckles. "I've been in court more times than you can count. Judges and prosecutors have swimming pools, tennis courts, and vacation homes to prove it."

His face grows serious.

"Are you a betting man, Jack?"

"You expect me to have a civil conversation with you? After beating your wife to death and *laughing* about it while eating breakfast? You're psychotic."

"The more you cooperate, the easier it'll go for you."

"You've already admitted you couldn't break Jill. You won't break me, either."

Bobby smiles. "Jill knew I loved her. She knew I'd show restraint. You won't get that type of coddling from me."

"Beating her to death is your idea of *coddling*?"

"Did you fuck my wife, Jack?"

"No."

"She said otherwise."

"You might have beaten a false confession out of her, but that doesn't change the facts."

"Were you planning to run away with her?"

"Fuck you, DiPiese. I've said all I'm going to say."

"You remember how we met, Jack? It was what, four years ago? I hired you to find a guy? I'd been searching for months with no luck. Took you what, two days?"

"It took me two hours. I *billed* you for two days."

Bobby chuckles. "Serves me right. That was what, four years ago?"

"Something like that."

"You happen to remember the man's name?"

"Todd Hardy."

"Who *does* that?" Bobby says. "Goes through high school, marries a college girl, has two kids, runs off and marries a guy in California, and takes the guy's last name?"

"Todd Hardy."

Bobby nods. "A moment ago I asked if you were a betting man. I had a reason for that. During the past two months you either found Jill two days ago, as you claim, or much sooner, which I suspect. But either way, you learned a lot by investigating her, and following her trail. My question is this:

how many different men would you guess my loving wife slept with during her life?"

"I couldn't care less."

"You'll want to re-think that, because I happen to know the exact number. And if you guess right, I'll spare your life. I'm not going to pay you the balance I owe, because you didn't actually return her, as promised. But you have my word. Get the exact number, and I'll spare your life. But if you guess wrong, it'll go badly for you."

"Five," Jack says.

Bobby looks surprised. "What made you say five? Did you have this conversation with Jill already?"

He did, in fact. But what he says is, "I'm right, aren't I?"

"We'll get to that in a minute. I'm just making sure that's your final answer. Bear in mind, she's thirty. *Was* thirty, if I'm being precise. And you said she was working in a strip joint."

"So?"

"Five seems a bit low, don't you think?"

"I'll stick with that number."

"Will you tell me the truth, Jack? Will you admit you fucked my wife? Will you give me that much?"

"I wouldn't give you the sweat off my dick."

A fourth goon walks in. "What do you want?" Bobby says.

"He's here. Your visitor."

"From the department?"

"Yeah. Carter."

"He brought his equipment?"

"Yeah."

Bobby says, "Take him to the den and wait with him."

When the goon leaves, Bobby turns his attention back to Jack. "Remember the jar I showed you last night?"

When Jack fails to respond, Bobby tells one of the goons to fetch it and place it on the table. When he does, Bobby says, "Rayburn, bring the tray I prepared. But be careful."

Rayburn leaves, comes back carrying a tray with four jars, all identical to the empty one on the table.

Except they aren't empty.

Each jar contains a pair of testicles.

Bobby picks up one of the jars and holds it so Jack can get a good look.

"Todd Hardy," Bobby says. "The guy you helped me find four years ago. Before he got married, had kids, ran off with his boyfriend from California...this was Jill's first boyfriend. They were high school sweethearts. She made it all through high school without getting laid, then this bastard slipped it to her the night they graduated."

He frowns. "These nuts were in my wife's mouth when she was a teenager."

He places the jar back on the tray and picks up the second one.

"Colton Boyd, college student. Lacrosse player. Big man on campus. Wealthy family. This piece of shit was the love of her life. He used her, cheated on her, dumped her. You know the type? Think they're better than everyone else? I crushed his feet and fed him to my hogs."

He studies Colton's nuts a while, then says, "I've had these a long time."

He puts the jar down, picks up the next one. "Professor Owen Wolfe." Of all the pricks who fucked my wife, this was the worst. A fuckin' professor. He came at her the week Colton dumped her, which happened to be the same week her father died. Talk about a Satan double-header! I figured this guy must have brass balls for taking advantage of a young, broken-hearted coed like that, but as you can see, they're nothing special."

He puts the jar beside the others and says, "I've got the professor's dick in another jar. It's my only dick." He looks at Jack, then adds, "So far."

"The nuts of her fourth lover are attached to my lower abdomen," he says. "And although I was fourth in line, I'm proud to say I'll go to my grave being Jill's *last* lover."

"With any luck you'll go there soon," Jack says.

Bobby holds up the last jar. "Lover number five," he says. "I never told you this, but Jill ran away once before. Guy's name was Wisby. Marcus Wisby. Rayburn, tell Jack who Marcus was."

Rayburn says, "Your driver."

Bobby says, "You *believe* that shit? My fuckin' *driver!* She gave it up to this bastard for a fuckin' *ride!*"

Jack says, "Did they run off together?"

"No. Wisby drove her to Baton Rouge, fucked her, drove back alone. I didn't find out what he'd done till I beat it out of her."

Jack says, "How long was she gone?"

"Three days. And you wouldn't believe the beating I gave her for *that* shit."

"I expect she'd say it was worth it."

Bobby's expression stays the same, but his eyes go reptilian. "Rayburn?"

"Yes, sir?"

"Put this nut tray back where you found it, then get Carter, and tell him to bring his shit in here."

When Rayburn leaves, Bobby tells his other goons to clear the table, except for the empty jar. By the time they finish, Rayburn returns with a short, curly-haired guy with thick glasses who looks like he plays football, basketball, and soccer, every day of his life—on X-box.

Bobby says, "Jack, this is Carter. Can you look at his equipment and guess his job with the parish police department?"

"He gives lie detector tests."

"That's right. Take a seat, Carter, and hook him up."

While Carter gets the machine ready, Bobby goes on a texting jag. He's working so furiously, no one wants to interrupt him. Finally he looks up and says, "You're ready?"

Carter nods. He's been ready for ten minutes.

"Can you leave us a minute?"

Carter stands, Rayburn escorts him out the room.

Bobby says, "Okay, Jack, last chance. I asked you how many lovers Jill's had in her life and you said five, which was the correct answer before you came into the picture. You say you didn't have sex with her, and if the lie detector agrees, you get to keep your nuts. Does that sound fair?"

Jack says, "Maybe I'll tell Carter about the jars and what you did to Jill."

"Tell him whatever you think is worth dying for, because anything you say beyond answering his questions will cost you your life. It's up to you, Jack. But if you want my opinion, I think you'd be making a poor trade, since Carter's heavily on my payroll."

Jack has to give Bobby credit where credit's due. It's ingenious, having the police lie detector guy in his pocket. He can find out everything the police know but can't use in court. That's tremendous leverage for a guy like Bobby.

Bobby says, "I'll ask you one last time. Tell me the truth about what happened, *how* it happened, and why. Tell me that, and I'll spare your life."

"You're saying you'll let me go if I tell you what happened?"

"No. I said I'd spare your life."

"What does that mean, exactly?"

"It means I'll chain you to my basement wall with the others, but I won't feed you to the hogs."

"The truth is I drove her to the place we met the four hunters. After killing them, I took one of the trucks and drove Jill to Hammond. I didn't know it at the time but one of the bullets from the explosion damaged the truck. By the time we got to Hammond, the truck was about to die on me. I stole a car and kidnapped the family that owned it, put them in the trunk, and started heading here. After a few miles on the highway, they kicked out the tail lights, and I was afraid we'd be stopped. I didn't want to get caught in the middle of a kidnapping, so I pulled off and got caught up in the Virgin Boat Festival. We abandoned the car and met a crazy lady who took us on horseback to a bait shop. The owner air-boated us to an airfield, and according to you, Mike flew Jill to Jackson instead of La Pierre."

Bobby pauses to absorb the data. Then says, "When did you fuck her?"

"I didn't."

Bobby picks up the empty jar, turns it in his hands a minute.

"Good story," he says. "Let's see if the lie detector backs you up."

Chapter 6

When the test is over, Carter shows Bobby the peaks he's circled that represent lies.

"Just so we're clear, when Jack said he never kissed my wife…"

"That was a lie."

"And when he said he never touched my wife's breasts?"

"That was a lie."

"And when he said he never had sex with her?"

"That was a lie."

"And when you asked it a different way, if he'd ever had intercourse with her, he said no, and…"

"That was also a lie."

"And when you asked if they had oral sex, he said no…"

"And that answer was truthful."

"And when he said he didn't know she was flying to Jackson?"

"That was a lie."

"And when he said they weren't planning to run away together?"

"That was also a lie."

"Could any of these be—what do you call them? False positives?"

"There's always a possibility of false positives. But this subject showed truthful answers to every control question you knew to be true."

"What's your degree of confidence in this particular test result?"

"Ninety to ninety-five percent."

Carter looks at the empty jar and says, "Is that for his nuts?"

Bobby says, "Thanks for your time, Carter."

Chapter 7

After Carter leaves, Bobby says, "Anything you'd like to say to me, Jack?"

"Yeah. The guy's a hack. Polygraphs are known to be accurate exactly sixty-one percent of the time."

"Don't be a sore loser, Jack."

"I never touched your wife."

Bobby imitates Carter's voice, saying, "...And that was a lie."

Jack frowns.

Bobby says, "I won't ask you to give me the details at this time. When it comes down to the nut-cutting, you'll tell me everything. Why the fuck are you smiling?"

It's true.

Jack's grinning like an idiot.

Bobby says, "This makes you happy? What, you always wanted to lose your nuts?"

"Marcus Wisby," Jack says. "Jill's fifth lover."

Bobby frowns. "What about him?"

Jack laughs. "It just hit me: Jill's alive. Not only is she alive, she was never here. Not last night, anyway."

"And you came to this conclusion how?"

"Marcus Wisby, your driver, and the cab driver from Jackson, Mississippi, Vick Wamby. I knew that was a bullshit story, when you said Wamby was on your payroll."

"Tell me."

"I *talked* to the fucking cab driver."

"So?"

"He was Iranian. I can't remember his name, but it sure as hell wasn't Vick Wamby!"

"Maybe I embellished that part."

"You embellished the whole fucking story, Bobby. She was never here last night. The whole thing was staged."

"Want to see her body?"

"Yeah. I'd love to see it. Let's go. Right now. Show me."

The two men stare each other down. Bobby says, "What makes you think it was staged?"

"When Jill ran off the first time you beat the shit out of her."

"So?"

"You taped that beating and replayed it for me last night, to get my reaction. Then you tried to use the whole killing Jill story to get me to confess."

"What about the lie detector guy?" Bobby says.

"Is he for real?"

"He is."

"Then he's a hack."

"The police department doesn't think so."

"The court system does."

"Let's not quibble about the validity of lie detectors," Bobby says. "What makes you think the beating you heard was taped from another time?"

"I notice you haven't denied it."

"I'm still at the 'how could you possibly believe that?' stage."

"During the beating last night, Jill kept saying, 'There's no one else! I've been faithful!'"

"So?"

"The first time she ran off you didn't know she had sex with Wisby until *after* you beat her up."

"So?"

"When the beating started, you didn't suspect Wisby. If you *had*, you would have asked if she fucked him and she would have said, "No." She would *not* have said 'There's no one else.' That's the answer to a different question."

"I can't follow your logic," Bobby says.

"She answered the question you asked. And when you asked it, you didn't know about Wisby. But last night you suspected she and I had sex. If she'd been here last night you would have asked, 'Did you fuck Jack Tallow?' and she would have said, 'No.' But she kept saying, 'There's no one else.' It's the answer to a different question. The one you asked the first time she ran away when you didn't have a specific person in mind. She wasn't here last night. Admit it."

Bobby pauses a while, then says, "Your explanation sucks. It was torture to my ears."

"But?"

"But you're right. She was never here. Like you said, her beating was taped from the first time. But don't act so smug. I made you cry. And I'm still going to cut off your nuts."

"At least I know Jill got away safely."

"You think?"

"I know."

Bobby unwraps his hands and tosses the gauze on the counter behind him with the dirty dishes. Then says, "Why do you assume I don't know exactly where she is?"

"If you knew where she was, you wouldn't have gone through this whole charade with me. You'd have brought her back and beat her up the way you planned."

"So if I told you that a half hour ago Jill was in a lake house on Leeds Road in Willow Lake, Arkansas, that belongs to a guy named Jack Russell, who happens to be *you*, what would you call that, a lucky guess?"

Jack's heart nearly stops.

Bobby says, "You know what I'd call it?"

"Synchronicity," Jack says.

Bobby smiles. "In another world, under different circumstances, I bet we'd be friends."

"You'd lose that bet."

Bobby shrugs. "Perhaps you're right. Look, I'm tired of dicking around. Are you ready to give up your nuts?"

"No."

"Just to show there are no hard feelings—no pun intended—I'll let you hang onto them till tomorrow night."

"Why so generous?"

"I want you to be completely lucid when the explosion takes place."

"What explosion?"

"All in good time, Jack."

He looks at his goons. "Rayburn? Clayton? Please help me escort Jack to the basement. Jack? You'll want to glance out the window, and at your watch, so you can remember the exact moment you saw daylight for the last time in your life."

He looks at his watch and thinks, *It's eleven-thirty. Last time I spoke to Jill was two-forty-five. She did what I told her to do—left without me and took a cab to the lake house. That would have been around four a.m. Seven-and-a-half hours ago.*

Chapter 8

Jill DiPiese.
Private Airfield, Jackson, Mississippi.
4:00 a.m.
Seven-and-a-half Hours Earlier.

After calling Jack's number twenty-six times without getting an answer, Jill tells the cabbie to take her to the Memphis airport as fast as possible. Once there, she enters the bathroom, washes her face, looks in the mirror. Wonders what she'd pay for a hairbrush, toothpaste and toothbrush. But all the shops are closed. She thinks about Jack and bursts into tears. After composing herself as best she can, she walks back out and flags the first cab in line.

"I'm Frank," he says.

Taking note of her swollen eyes, tear-streaked cheeks, filthy clothes, he asks, "Are you okay?"

"I'm not at my best, today, Frank. I'm...Emma. Emma Wilson."

He pauses, then says, "Where to, Emma?"

"Ever heard of Willow Lake, Arkansas?"

"Heard of it? Yeah. Been there? No, not yet. Is that where we're going?"

"Do you have time to take me that far? And help me run some errands when we arrive?"

"Of course."

"You're sure?"

"It's what I do, Emma."

Chapter 9

La Pierre, Louisiana.
Bobby's Basement.

"There aren't many basements in Louisiana," Bobby says, as they head down the steps. Then adds, "And there are none in the world like this one. Come, I'll give you the grand tour."

The basement is well-lighted, but musty. At the bottom of the steps there's a small sitting area, and two steel doors. One's in front of them, the other, to their right. Bobby removes a card from his pocket and slides it through a scanner. The first door clicks, and Bobby opens it, revealing a hall with twenty-four jail cells. As they walk down the hall, Bobby introduces Jack to the prisoners. Sounding more like a tour director than a fiend, he says, "First cell on the left belongs to Don Hess. Don, meet Jack."

Don hisses at him.

"That's Don's kid, Billy, on the right. Say hi, Billy."

Billy hisses.

Bobby says, "On the left is Don's wife, Blair. I'll give Blair a good fucking from time to time, just to annoy Don and Billy."

There are fourteen prisoners. Two men, eight women, four children. The children's ages range from approximately sixteen to early twenties. All heads have been completely shaved, and each prisoner hisses when Bobby commands. When they come to the end of the hall Bobby says, "You're probably wondering who these people are, am I right?"

Jack says nothing.

Bobby says, "You've heard of the Witness Protection Program?"

"What about it?"

"It's a federal program."

"So?"

"Most people don't know it's federal, not state. And there's a lot of hassle and red tape involved, and certain criteria needs to be met before they'll accept a witness or his family into the program. The bottom line, most witnesses don't get approved. Ask me where I'm going with this."

"Where are you going with this?"

"I know some unscrupulous prosecutors who want the witness's testimony so badly, they tell the families they've been accepted even when they weren't. They promise new identities, housing, living expenses, medical care, job training, and employment assistance in return for their testimony. That's where we come in. I get two of my guys to put on suits and pretend they're U.S. Marshals. We give them twenty-four hour protection in high-threat environments like pretrial conferences, court appearances, and trials. When the trials are over, my guys drive them here and I put them in cells."

He laughs. "Can you imagine the look on their faces? They're expecting this whole new life, and they wind up worse off than the guys they testified against!"

He laughs some more. Then says, "I usually sell the informant to the guys he testified against, and keep the wives and children. I fuck the females, and feed the males to my hogs on the Blood River."

"You have sex with their *children?*"

"Of course! But not till they're of age. I mean, what sort of monster do you think I am?"

"The kind who just admitted fucking the females."

"I'm not the heartless bastard you make me out to be. I make a point to celebrate every child's eighteenth birthday."

"You don't strike me as a cake and ice cream kind of guy."

"I celebrate in my own way. When girls turn eighteen, I pop their cherries. When boys turn eighteen, I crush their feet and toss them in the hog pen. Any other questions?"

"Why are they hissing at me?"

"We cut their vocal cords to keep the sound under control, and discourage communication between family members. We'll cut your cords, too, after the explosion."

They retrace their steps, go out the door, and Bobby runs his card through the scanner beside the second door. When it clicks, Bobby opens it and says, "This is where you'll be spending the rest of your life, unless I decide to turn you into hog meal."

This hall is identical to the first one, except shorter. It contains twelve jail cells. The last two are empty.

"There are currently three noteworthy guests in this wing," Bobby says. "First on the left is the dickless wonder, Professor Owen Wolfe. The cell beside him belongs to Todd Hardy. Across from him is my old driver, Marcus Wisby. Take a good look at Todd and Marcus's private area, because that's what yours will look like in a couple of days. Like a twig without the berries."

Jack feels a pinch in his right shoulder, but before he can react, his legs give way. Within seconds he's completely paralyzed.

"Don't be upset, Jack. Over the years we've learned it's easier to strip our prisoners when they're drugged. The effects will wear off in a couple of hours."

Bobby's goons strip Jack and chain his neck to the wall. Then Bobby says, "We've given you five feet of slack in the chain, which allows you to stand, sit, or lie down beside the wall. But we can tighten the chain and force you to stand whenever we want. Sometimes we'll tighten it for spite, sometimes for fun, but we always tighten it when you misbehave. You might think you can just relax your legs and hang yourself, but we've learned it doesn't work that way. Human nature being what it is, your legs will find a way to save you every time. We'll feed you once a day and remove your shit bucket twice a day. If you spill the bucket, you don't eat that day. Sometimes you'll spill the bucket on purpose, just to break the monotony. We understand it, but you won't want to make a habit of it. Twice a week we hose you down, and if you've been cooperative that week, we'll let you use soap. The barber comes in once a week to shave you, including head, underarms, and private area. I plan to let you keep your vocal cords and nuts till after the explosion tomorrow night, because what I've got planned is huge, and I want you to be a part of it. But if you cry or make any noises louder than a bowel movement before then, we'll cut your cords and nuts ahead of schedule."

Bobby starts to leave, then says, "It's your call, Jack, but if I were you, I'd enjoy my dick as much as possible the next two days."

With that, he closes the cell door, locks it, then he and his goons walk away.

Chapter 10

"Jack, pay attention," Bobby says. "I think you'll be able to appreciate this."

It takes Jack a moment to realize he's not dreaming. Bobby's actually sitting on a folding chair in the hall in front of his cell. He wonders how it's possible only a day-and-a-half has passed since he began his imprisonment. To Jack it feels like a week. He assumed Bobby got busy with one of his many other nefarious activities, and forgot to mutilate him.

Bobby says, "You've got some experience with explosives, right? I mean, you blew up those hunters a couple nights ago."

Jack starts to speak, but nothing comes out. He swallows, clears his throat, and tries again. "I know a little," he says. "Why are you asking?"

"Have you ever heard of a double bomb?"

"No."

Bobby says, "I'm not sure exactly how it works, but as I understand it, a master bomb-builder can fill a canister with eighty-pounds of powdered aluminum, and a fuel substance, and use a scatter charge to detonate it."

"That's just a conventional explosive, with aluminum powder. What's the purpose of the powder?"

"The first explosion creates a mushroom cloud of aluminum powder. Then, a guy on the ground uses a rocket launcher to fire a small warhead at the cloud, and the cloud somehow makes the second explosion exponentially more powerful than it would have been on its own. Does that make sense?"

"You're talking about some sort of FAE."

"What does that mean?"

"Fuel-Air Explosive. There's a more technical term, but I can't remember it."

Jack pauses. He didn't expect to have a conversation with Bobby before having his vocal cords removed, nor did he desire one. And yet, here he is, chatting away like an old woman in a nursing home. Why? Because it suddenly dawned on him this could be the last conversation he'll ever have, using his voice. More importantly, it could be a chance to find out what's happened to Jill.

Bobby says, "I want your opinion on how much damage this type of explosive could do."

"It depends on several factors."

"Such as?"

"The quality of ingredients, the skill of the bomb-builder, the height of the initial detonation, the diameter of the cloud, the size of the warhead..."

"Assume the bomb-builder's top notch. Assume the first bomb detonates a hundred feet above the target, and the warhead is equal to thirteen pounds of TNT."

"That's a formidable weapon. What's the target?"

"Your lake house."

"*What?*" Jack can't see his face, of course, but knows it just turned white. When he's able to find his voice again, he says, "*Why?*"

"The why is *my* business," Bobby says. "But I'll tell you the how. Two hours ago the bomb-builder loaded an eighty pound canister to the bottom of Mike's crop duster. In half an hour or less, Mike's going to fly over your lake house and pull a lever that will disengage the canister. If all goes according to plan, it'll self-detonate a hundred feet above your home. Then, my man on the ground—the same one who saved Jill's life two hours ago—will—" He pulls a piece of paper from his pocket and reads, "...use a rocket launcher to fire a thermobaric warhead at the target."

Jack stares straight ahead. Thermobaric. That's the term he couldn't remember.

Bobby says, "I call it a double bomb. You know, keep it simple, right?"

Jack slumps against the back wall of his cell. "Why would you possibly want to do this?"

"Like I said, that's *my* business. But the short version is I'm considering using explosives for personal gain. I've been working with an expert bomb-builder for months. The choice of target is quite recent, though, and I have you to thank for that. So this is a test, to see how well the weapon works. And it offers the added benefit of being a fun way to kill Jill."

"You're going to blow her up? That's your plan?"

"Yup. Cool, huh?"

"More like insane."

Bobby chuckles, then says, "The last thing that'll go through Jill's mind before she dies? Her ass!"

"That's an old joke."

Bobby shrugs. "What do you expect? I'm an old man."

"I don't think you understand the magnitude of what you're doing. A weapon like that could destroy everything within a hundred yards of the target! Other homes. Innocent people."

"Tough shit."

Jack stares at him with total contempt. "You're a pig of a man."

Bobby grins. Says, "Oink!"

"Fuck you."

"Don't be bitter, Jack. No one likes a bitter prisoner."

"I'd be a lot less bitter if I could keep my nuts and vocal cords."

"That's not going to happen, sport. You understand *why*, don't you?"

"Tell me. I'd like to hear the words as they leak out of your foul, sadistic, cesspool of a mouth."

"It's the ultimate torture, Jack. You, sitting in this cell for the rest of your life with no hope of ever seeing the light of day. Nothing to do all day, all night, day after day. Guys on death row have it ten times better than you! They can talk to family members, guards, their attorneys...they can dream, hope, eat a variety of food...and they can jack off. Not you, Jack. You'll get the same meal at the same time every day for the rest of your life. You won't be able to complain or cry out in anger or frustration, because the only sound you'll be able to make is a hiss. And your hiss will sound like everyone else's. You'll retreat into your mind, like prisoners in solitary confinement, except that *those* prisoners can think of the women they've been with, or wanted to be with, and can express those thoughts physically. But you'll avoid those thoughts, Jack, because your dick won't work. You'll be amazed how frustrating that'll be when you're sitting in a cell twenty-four hours a day. I'm taking *everything* from you: your time, your life, your hope for a better future, your ability to communicate, your sexual thoughts, your ability to pleasure yourself, your will to live."

Jack decides not to tell Bobby that men can lose their nuts and still get erections and experience orgasms. This, according to Jack's best friend from college, who got testicular cancer, lost his nuts, but claimed he could still perform.

Jack says, "You're the man, Bobby. You can take all that away from me. But you know what you can't do?"

"What's that, sport?"

"You can't make Jill love you."

"Her loss."

"We both know whose loss it is," Jack says.

"Jesus, Jack. Have you *no* pride? You *do* know she was using you, right? In her eyes you're no better than Wisby, my driver. All she wanted was to get away. And as for Jill living in a hillbilly tourist town in Bum Fuck, Arkansas?" He laughs. "She wouldn't have lasted a month. And if you knew her at all, you'd know that."

Jack waits it out while Bobby continues putting him down. But when he says, "You actually made me feel sorry for you yesterday morning," Jack says, "I doubt that."

"It's true. When I told you Jill agreed to come back if I let you go? You actually *believed* me!" He laughs. "How *pathetic*. What a *sap* you are!"

He laughs some more.

Jack says, "You mentioned your guy saved her life two hours ago?"

"Yeah, that's right."

"How?"

"Remember our talk about synchronicity?"

"Coincidences are like conspiracy theories. If they're on your mind, you find them everywhere."

"I'll give that some thought, Jack. In the meantime, see if you agree *this* is a coincidence. Remember Abbie Rhodes, from Willow Lake?"

The expression on his face says he does.

"What about her?"

"Two hours ago her husband Darryl attacked Jill in your front yard because, according to him, you fucked his wife. Get the coincidence? At the same time he's punishing Jill because you fucked *his* wife, I'm punishing *you* for fucking *my* wife!"

Jack closes his eyes, thinking *Poor Jill. She'd have been safer with Bobby than me.*

Bobby says, "Don't worry. My guy put a bullet in Darryl's forehead. Now half the town's in your front yard. Neighbors, cops, technicians...if my bomb guy's calculations are right, we're going to wipe out half the town's population tonight."

"You're telling me this for a reason," Jack says.

"What do you mean?"

"There's something you want me to do in return for not killing Jill. It's why you wanted me completely lucid tonight.

Whatever it is, I'll do it. Spare Jill's life and I'll do whatever you want."

Bobby's face shows amusement. "You'll do anything?"

"Yes."

"Would you kill yourself?"

"Yes, of course."

"Kill a child?"

"Yes."

"Have sex with a goat?"

"A goat?"

"You said 'anything.'"

Jack frowns in disgust. "Spare Jill and I'll do anything you say."

"Tell me you'll have sex with a goat and all the male prisoners here. Wait. Let me tape this." He presses a button on his cell phone. Then says, "Okay. What's your name?"

"Jack Tallow."

"Jack, tell me what you're willing to do if I let Jill go."

Jack says, "I'll have sex with a goat and all the male prisoners here."

Bobby laughs till his sides hurt. Then he clicks off the recording app and says, "Are you listening to yourself, Jack?"

"Yeah. And I keep hearing myself say I'll do anything, but I don't hear you telling me what it'll take."

"Kill Jill."

"What?"

"Would you kill Jill?"

He pauses. "Yes."

"Why? Because you think you can kill her more humanely than me?"

"No. But if I kill her myself at least the other people in Willow Lake will live."

"What, I'm supposed to think you're a wonderful guy now? A real humanitarian?"

"I don't give a shit what you think of me."

"You say you'll do anything," Bobby says.

"That's right."

"Would you trade places with Jill?"

"What do you mean?"

"Would you be willing to walk out of here a free man, knowing Jill would have to take your place?"

"I'm not sure I understand."

"I don't need *you* to bring Jill back. I could have my man on the ground do it tonight. But believe me when I say I'll treat her worse than the others. I won't just let her rot, I'll punish her in ways you can't even comprehend. What if I bring her back, put her on this chair, and force you to tell her the reason she's going to be in a jail cell for the rest of her life is because I traded your freedom for her captivity. Would you still want me to spare her life?"

"No."

Bobby laughs. "That was fun, don't you think?"

"What do you mean?"

"I was just fucking with you. My man can't waltz in there and remove her with all those people milling about. There are a hundred of them crawling all over the neighborhood. You thought I was telling you all this for a reason? I was. But only because I wanted to gloat, like any respectable movie villain would do. No, Jack, there's nothing I want from you. Except to make you feel utterly powerless, like I felt when Jill stopped loving me and there was nothing I could do about it. And of course I want you to experience the agony of losing your home, your neighbors, and your new girlfriend. I want you to live with the knowledge that if you'd simply kept your dick in your pants and brought her back, like you were *paid* to do, none of this would have happened. I'm telling you all this and keeping you lucid because I want you to share this moment with me. You and I will experience Jill's death together. And this memory will be firmly etched in your mind when my doctor removes your nuts and vocal cords."

He puts his phone on speaker and presses a button.

Jack hears the phone ring, hears a man answer, "Decker."

Bobby says, "Can you talk?"

"Yeah," Decker says. "I'm in position. No one can hear me."

"I've got Jack Tallow on speaker phone."

"He's with you? At your place?"

"Yeah. Have you heard from Mike the Pilot?"

"We've been in contact."

"Tell Jack what's going to happen to his lake house."

"Mike's going to fly over the house, drop the canister. When it detonates, the aluminum powder and fuel will form a mushroom cloud that'll mix with atmospheric oxygen, and fall like rain on all people and structures within the blast radius. Then I'll fire a warhead to detonate the cloud, and create a blast wave strong enough to destroy everything within the initial radius."

"You used the word 'destroy.'"

"That's right."

"Can you give Jack a precise description of what you mean?"

"The lake house will be completely decimated, including the basement foundation, to a depth of at least six feet. Surrounding houses will suffer massive damage."

"And the people in the house and yard?"

"In the simulated version, most would become human fireballs. Those furthest away would suffer critical, if not fatal, injuries, including ruptured lungs, blindness, burst eardrums, extensive third-degree burns..."

"Will we be able to hear the screams?"

Decker pauses a moment before saying, "What screams?"

"From the wounded people."

"Hopefully there won't be any."

"What do you mean?"

"Mike's parked on your airfield in Memphis, waiting for my call. Which he won't get till all the gawkers have cleared the area."

"What are you *talking* about? You said we could wipe out half the town tonight."

"I was explaining the explosive force. We *could* kill most of those people tonight. But we're not going to."

"We're not?"

"No, Mr. Dee. We're not."

"Why?"

"Because I don't work that way."

"You killed Darryl tonight. And you agreed to kill Jill."

"That's different."

Bobby thinks about it a minute, then says, "You're still planning to kill Jill, though, right?"

"I said I would."

"And that means?"

"She's as good as dead. You have my word. She won't escape."

"You're certain she's in the house?"

"I got a visual on her through the window a short while ago."

"Could she have slipped out the back?"

"Not hardly."

"Why not?"

"For one thing, there are several people in the house with her. For another, I would've seen her. I'm in the water, behind Jack's house."

"You're in the *water*? What about your equipment? Your rocket launcher?"

"Everything's in the bass boat."

"I don't' understand."

"I hid the rocket launcher and sniper rifle in the hold of a bass boat and drove it to the edge of the peninsula hours ago. I took my rifle up the hill to use my scope as a spotter to give Mike coordinates and terrain. Saw Darryl and his wife pull into Jack's driveway. When Jill showed up after jogging, I moved in close enough to hear their confrontation. Darryl came at her, and I killed him."

"You should have shot Jill, too."

"You hired me to blow her up, not shoot her."

"Just so we're clear. If she escapes from the house before you blow it up—"

"I'll hunt her down, kill her, cut her head off, and bring it to you."

"Perfect. Where are you now?"

"A quarter-mile from shore, hanging on the side of the boat."

"How the fuck can you fire a rocket launcher while treading water?"

"I'll prop it on the side of the boat, and fire from here."

"What if you miss?"

"Ray Charles couldn't miss the target Mike's going to make."

"Still, you're a quarter-mile away," Bobby says. "I'd feel better if you moved closer."

"Any closer and I'll be part of the barbecue."

"Well, can you *see* anything? I mean, it's dark out back, right? How would you be able to tell if Jill makes a run for it?"

"I'm wearing night vision goggles. Anyone comes out the back, I see them."

"I'm going to want visual confirmation of Jill's death."

Decker pauses. "That's going to be hard to do."

"Why?"

"I could drive the boat to shore, but I'd have to search through the flames and rubble."

"You should have time to do that, if everyone in the neighborhood is dead or dying."

"The neighborhood casualties will be limited to Jill and whoever else is still in the house when I fire the warhead. But they'll be carbon by the time I get there. I won't be able to tell men from women."

"I don't want her getting away."

"She's not going anywhere. The sheriff has been questioning her. He's not going to let her out of his sight."

"I still want you to check the house afterward."

"Because?"

"The bitch always seems to find a way to fuck up my plans."

Decker sighs. "I'll do my best."

"What about Mike the Pilot?"

"If you still want him eliminated, I'll shoot before he clears the blast area. If you want him alive, I'll wait an extra twenty seconds before firing."

"Mike's a good man," Bobby says, "but he knows too much. Shoot early, and call me when it's over."

"Okay. When I fire the warhead I'll film the results and stream them to you."

"Sounds like a plan."

They end the call.

Jack says, "Don't do this, Bobby. It's mass murder."

"You're turning into a nag, Jack."

"And you're turning into a terrorist."

Bobby says, "Can I be honest? You're not much fun to be around."

"Sorry if I'm ruining your big moment."

"Are you *always* like this? Because I've gotta tell you, the sound of your voice is making a big stink in my ears."

Bobby presses a button on his phone. When someone answers he says, "Is the doctor here yet? Good. Bring him on down." He listens a moment, then says, "Yes, of *course* I'm going to watch. I *always* watch."

Part Four:

A GREASE PEN, A HOG PEN,
A TOW TRUCK, AND A PLAN

Chapter 1

Leeds Road, Willow Lake, Arkansas.
Present Day, Present Time.

Bobby's man on the ground, Ryan Decker, removes his night vision goggles and places them in the boat. Then gives Mike the Pilot the go-ahead, which means Decker has thirty seconds to get the rocket launcher in position.

More than enough time.

Mike flies over Jack's house, disengages the canister, and the initial bomb detonates just as it was programmed to do.

No surprise there, Decker knows his shit.

He'd love to take a few seconds to marvel at the mushroom cloud, but since he needs to blow Mike out of the sky, he can't spare the time. He fires the warhead, tosses the rocket launcher in the boat, and ducks underneath, just in case he miscalculated the distance.

He didn't.

The explosion rocks the sky. As predicted, when Decker surfaces, he sees half the neighborhood in flames. Jack's house has been leveled, as have the vacant houses on both sides. To the left, several other vacant homes are on fire. If he had done it Bobby's way, dozens of bystanders would be dead, dozens more would be in flames, running and hopping about like fireflies.

Ryan gets his cell phone from the boat, takes a short video, texts it to Bobby. Ten minutes later, he calls from the blast site.

Bobby says, "I got the video. Fuckin' *amazing!*"

Decker says, "I'm standing behind Jack's house. The area's too hot for me to get closer right now, but I have some information for you."

"Will it make me happy?"

"I think so. Is Jack Tallow still with you?"

"He is, but he's unconscious. I just had his vocal cords removed."

Decker pulls the phone away from his ear and stares at it a moment in disbelief. Then puts it back to his ear and says, "*Why?*"

"I gave him a choice of losing his nuts or his vocal cords."

"And he chose his vocal cords?"

"Surprisingly, no. He chose to lose his nuts. So I took his vocal cords. I'll take his nuts in a few days. Give him something to look forward to. Cool, huh?"

"I'm at a bomb site, remember?"

"Right. Sorry. What's the good news?"

"Jack's house had a secret room."

"What do you mean?"

"It's a fall-away lot to the lake. He built a secret room beneath the main floor that's hidden behind the retaining wall."

"How do you know?"

"Because the blast took out the ceiling and front wall."

"Why's that good news for me?"

"Your wife was in the secret room when the bomb went off."

"No shit? That's great! Wait. You're sure it's her?"

"Yeah, I'm sure. The secret room goes under the ground on one end, and butts up against the retaining wall that faces the lake. There's a metal door below it, and maybe Jack had a way to use the door as an escape route. But if he did, Jill didn't know about it, because she's still in there. It's freaky the way the blast affected the secret room."

"What do you mean?"

"It's like I'm looking at the back half of a kid's doll house. Half the secret room is still intact. That's the part that was partially underground. Jill's lying on her side on the cot like nothing happened, except that most of the organs that used to be inside her are splattered all over the room."

"You're sure she's dead?"

"Trust me. Her body imploded from the power of the blast. If I could get closer, I'd drag her out and throw what's left of her on the ground and send you a photograph."

"Can you try?"

"Not to complain, but I'm still at the bomb site, remember? I originally planned to haul ass after firing the warhead. Now you've had me drive the boat ashore, engage in a discussion about severed nuts and vocal cords, and I've taken the time to find and positively identify your wife's body, which I managed to do only because of the secret room. And yes, she's thoroughly and completely dead. Had she been anywhere else I wouldn't have been able to ID her. But I'd prefer not to take the time to work my way into the wreckage and pull her out. It's a very dangerous area. Also, I wouldn't have time to get her DNA off me."

"You could make it look like you're searching for survivors."

"True, but there's the issue of my bass boat tied to what's left of Jack's boat dock. Not to mention my sniper's rifle and rocket launcher are in the boat, and I have to get them and myself out of the area."

Bobby sighs. "Okay, leave her there. But photograph what you can, and send it to me."

"Will do."

Decker takes some pictures of the general area and forwards them to Bobby, knowing in advance his cell phone can't provide definitive details because he's too far away, it's dark, and there's smoke and pockets of fire everywhere.

Decker turns off his phone and removes the battery so no one can trace him. Then he runs to the front yard, searches to make sure no one else was killed or injured in the blast. He sees no one in the yard, but there's a man and two women lying by the side of the road a short distance away. They're rolling around, disoriented, but generally unhurt.

He recognizes one of them. Abbie Rhodes. Abbie says, "Emma Wilson must've flashed her tits again."

The young man says, "My parents run the grocery store."

Decker assumes the third woman is Milly Reston, town gossip.

Decker flips them onto their stomachs, pulls down their pants, takes a black grease pen from his pocket and writes the letters BWC on their asses. After photographing his work, he runs to the dock, jumps in the boat, pushes off. Fires up the motor and says, 'Bobby thinks you're dead."

"Thanks, Ryan," Jill says. "I owe you."

Chapter 2

Thirty Minutes Earlier...

Sheriff Cox wants Jill to provide Jack's phone number?

It's over.

The yard's crawling with people, and there are at least five others in the house. Jill was lucky to make it into the closet without being detected. There was a terrifying moment when she was completely vulnerable after sliding the freezer away from the wall. As she scrambled behind it in the dark she lost her shoe. She thought about leaving it in the closet, but doing so would be like painting an arrow that points to her location. She had to go back and find it, put it on, and start over.

And somehow she made it.

She must have been crazy to think Jack's stupid lake house idea would work. Nor did Jack do her any favors by failing to mention he fucked the backwoods child bride Abbie

Rhodes, who was basically half-receptacle, half-punching bag for her primitive Neanderthal husband, Darryl.

Jesus, Jack. Could you really be that careless with Abbie? This is a small town. Everyone knows everything.

Jill has no idea who killed Darryl, but it had to be someone connected to Bobby.

Which means she's no longer safe.

Not that she had much of a chance to live a quiet, happy life in the first place. Coming here without Jack instantly raised the sheriff's suspicions. It took him less than a day to determine her ID was fake.

Sheriff Cox said the deputy's going to be stationed up on the hill out front?

Perfect!

Because the last thing Jack mentioned about the secret room was the small trap door under the cot. You move the cot, lift the door, and drop six feet to the concrete floor of the storage shed. Then you slip out the metal door, run to the water, and swim the fuck out of here.

So she does.

Except that when she opens the storage shed door, she runs smack into Milly Reston, the snoopy lady who brought her the broccoli casserole.

"Jesus, Emma!" Milly says. "You scared me half to death!"

"Sorry."

"The Sheriff's been looking for you for more than an hour."

"What a coincidence! I was just looking for *him*!"

"He thinks you ran away."

"That's silly. Where would I go? I need to tell him something amazing. Something I never would've found if not for you."

"What?"

"Jack's secret place."

"*Really?* You found something?"

"You have no idea, Milly!"

"Tell me!"

"You'd have to see it to believe it."

"Show me!"

Jill opens the door to the shed and points to the open trap door. "Jack has a secret room, filled with treasures and detailed information about half the people in town!"

"I've got to see it!"

"Well..."

"No. I'm serious. I have to see it. Can you give me a boost?"

"What about Sheriff Cox?"

"*Fuck* Sheriff Cox!"

Jill pretends to think it over. Then says, "Okay. I guess I can give you ten minutes before telling Sheriff Cox."

"You're a peach, Emma!"

Jill says, "There's a light on the left wall, by the built-in ladder."

She boosts Milly high enough to gain access to the secret room.

As Milly hoists herself up, Jill says, "Have fun snooping!"

"You know I will!" Milly says.

She closes the trap door, and Jill runs to the edge of the water, starts wading in...

...And hears a man whisper, "Jill! Over here!"

Chapter 3

The man says his name's Ryan Decker, and he's the one who shot Darryl. He says, "Stay quiet, and I'll get you out of here safely."

"I'll die before I let you take me back to Bobby!" Jill says.

She starts wading toward shore, but stops cold when Decker says, "I'm a friend of Jack's."

She turns toward him. "Where's Jack? Why didn't *he* come?"

Decker tells her to hang onto the side of the boat and be quiet, and he'll take her across the lake.

Except that when they get a quarter mile from the house he tells her the truth. He's not here because of Jack, but because of Bobby. "I don't work for your husband," he says, "but I'm *affiliated* with him."

"What do you mean?"

"I'm doing a job for him tonight, but I'm not on his payroll."

"What job?"

"He hired me to blow up Jack's house."

"*What?* You came here to *kill* me?"

"*He* thinks so. But if I thought so, you'd be dead."

She pauses a moment, then says, "You killed Darryl?"

"Yes."

"You saw my boobs?"

"Not really."

"Either you did or you didn't."

"I did. But I didn't let it affect my aim."

"How did you know I'd run to the lake just now?"

"I didn't, but I'm not surprised. Bobby said you always find a way to fuck up his plans."

"How's Jack involved in all this?"

"He's not."

"So you lied about being his friend?"

"Yes." He pauses, then says, "We'd probably be friends if I knew him. It's just that..."

"You don't."

"Right."

"You deliberately lied to me."

"Yes. But only because I didn't want you to run off. Your only chance to get away is with me."

She says, "Where's Jack?"

"Bobby's got him."

"Shit! I knew it. Who turned him in, the crop duster guy?"

"Yeah, Mike. I'm going to blow him up in a few minutes."

"Excuse me?"

Ryan starts to answer, then says, "There's too much to explain. Here's what you need to know. Jack's not going to make it, but you are."

"Is he alive?"

"For the moment."

"Can you save him?"

"No. I'm sorry."

"*Don't take me back, Ryan!*"

"Quiet down! Sound carries over water."

"Don't take me back to La Pierre," she repeats, in a lower voice.

"I wouldn't do that. Not after what happened last time."

"What do you mean?"

"I'm the one Bobby hired to find you the first time you ran away. I tracked you down and told him where you were hiding. I think the reason Bobby hired Jack is because I was busy with this bomb project."

They cling to the side of the boat quietly for a minute, then Decker says, "If I knew he was going to beat you like that I never would have let him get his hands on you."

"Who told you about the beating?"

"He did. After Jack found you."

"Do you know anything about Jack?"

"No. And I'm sorry things didn't work out. But..."

His voice trails off.

"But what?"

"I think Jack did a lousy job with this whole thing. I guess he found you early, fell in love with you, decided at the last possible second to let you go. Is that right?"

She starts crying.

"It's okay," Decker says.

"No, it's not. He's going to die, and it's all my fault."

"It's Bobby's fault. And Jack's, for not having a better plan to protect you."

She sighs. 'He's a good guy, Ryan."

She cries some more.

Decker waits a respectful amount of time, then says, "I need to tell you how this is going down in a few minutes. Wait. Who's that?"

"Where?"

"Lady, coming out of the storage room."

"Milly Reston, town gossip."

They watch Milly walk around the house, toward the front yard.

Decker says, "That is one lucky woman, assuming she leaves the property. Anyone else in the house?"

"I don't think so."

"Good."

Chapter 4

Post-Explosion.
Present Time.

Decker powers up the boat, drives it across the lake, and runs it aground in a remote area. He and Jill get out, Decker places the weapons by a tree and scrubs the boat and guns with antibacterial wipes. He tells Jill to wait for him, then pushes the boat back into the water and drives it a hundred yards out, sets it adrift, and swims back to her.

He grabs the guns, they walk to his SUV.

"My clothes are wet with lake water," Jill says.

"So?"

"I don't want to ruin your seats."

"It's okay. It's a rental car."

They're quiet till they hit the main road, at which point Jill says, "I know you spoke to Bobby on the phone. Did he say anything about Jack?"

Decker bites his lip. "How close are you two?"

"He was hoping we'd start a new life together."

"And you?"

"I agreed to give it a try."

"In return for not taking you back?"

"Yes."

"Think you could have done it?"

"Here in Willow Lake?" She thinks a moment, then sighs. "Probably not. But I would have tried like hell." She hesitates a beat, then says, "Is he dead?"

"Yes."

"Bobby killed him?"

"He cut Jack's vocal cords so he couldn't scream."

"And killed him?"

"Yeah."

Decker knows that's not completely true, but figures it'll be better for Jill to believe it.

They ride in silence a long time. When they pass the first exit to Memphis, she says, "Jack deserved better."

Decker takes the airport exit, but turns right instead of left. Toward the airport hotel, not the rental car return. Moments later he pulls into the hotel parking lot.

"What're you doing?" she says.

"It just struck me you never asked where I was going. You just got in the car and rode with me all the way to Memphis."

She shrugs. "I have no place to go. Now that Bobby thinks I'm dead, I suppose I can go anywhere."

"You should probably get a new ID."

She says nothing.

Decker says, "You know how to do that?"

"Not really."

"Do you need some money?" he says.

"No. Jack gave me some."

"You'll want to stop using his credit card."

"Right."

"Um...you're aware the credit card you've been using says Tallow instead of Russell, right?"

Despite the tears in her eyes, she chuckles. "Jack was better at finding people than hiding from them."

"His paper trail was easy to follow. He did a good job with the house. I'll give him that. But the land deed?"

She looks at him, waits for him to say it.

"Jack Russell's loan was guaranteed by...Jack Tallow."

She smiles. "I miss him already."

Decker says, "I'm not a good man."

Jill says, "No shit?"

"Yeah, you know that. But all this time we've been together, whether in the water or driving here from Willow Lake—you never said a word about the innocent people who lost their properties tonight."

"No one's innocent, Ryan."

Maybe it's her soulful eyes, or the hint of a smile that plays on her lips. Maybe it's her delicate voice, or the way it comes at him like whispers through a keyhole. Maybe it's because she's got to start over from scratch, and doesn't know where to begin. Or maybe it's her beautiful face and killer body that makes him say, "You can travel with me if you like."

She looks at him as if she has no idea what her answer will be. But eventually says, "I'd feel very safe with you...until I didn't."

"I'm not sure what that means," he says.

"It means I'm drawn to men who let me down hard."

He nods. "That, I understand."

"You're going to build more bombs."

"Yes."

"For Bobby?"

"Probably not. But I have plans."

"Tell me."

"You'll think I'm insane."

Jill says, "I'm a looner."

"What's that?"

"I'm sexually attracted to balloons."

"Balloons?"

"That's right. Your turn."

"I'm the commander of an urban army."

"What's that?"

"You'll see."

"How will I know when I see it?"

"Look for the letters BWC."

"What's that mean?"

"Because We Can."

"I don't understand."

"That's okay. I don't expect you to."

They look through the windshield a minute, as if waiting for a light to change. Then he says, "Is there anything I can do for you before I return the car?"

"How much time do you have?"

"Four hours."

"It would be nice to get out of these wet clothes."

He says, "I can think of several ways to accomplish that."

"Pick one that involves saving Jack," she says.

"What do you mean?"

"He's still alive. I can feel it."

"That's bullshit."

She looks at him. Then says, "He's alive, and you lied to me."

Decker sighs. "I *did* lie. Again. But only because I thought it would be easier for you."

"Or perhaps you thought it would be easier for you to get in my pants."

He shrugs. "Either way, Jack's doomed."

"Help me save him."

"I can't."

She opens the passenger door, starts to get out.

Decker says, "You're not in love with him."

"That's true. It never got that far. But I love his attitude."

"His *attitude?*"

She smiles. "It might be misguided, but Jack's the most forgiving, the most confident, the most optimistic person I've ever met. No matter how bad it gets for him, he always believes things are going to work out."

"He's your Don Quixote, you're his Dulcinea."

She shrugs. "I've been called worse."

"You can't spend the rest of your life fucking balloons and crazy people."

Jill pauses a moment, then says, "Have fun blowing up the world, Ryan."

She exits the car, closes the door, starts walking toward the hotel.

Decker starts the car, pulls up beside her, says, "You can't save him, Jill. No one can."

"I know."

"I'm smarter," he says. "Tougher. More practical than Jack. And you are, too. You can see that, can't you?"

"The jury's still out on all that. But he's certainly a better *person* than we are."

"How so?"

She stops walking, turns to face him. "If I asked Jack to save you from Bobby, you know what he'd say?"

"He'd probably say 'Yes.'"

"He would, indeed. But even *more* important, if I asked is it *possible* to save you, he'd say, 'Of course!'"

"Which proves he's a fool."

"He just might surprise you, Ryan."

"I don't think so."

"You don't know him."

"I don't need to. I know Bobby. So do you."

She smiles. "You know what I think?"

He waits.

She says, "I think the world needs more people like Jack and fewer like you and me."

"You're never going to see him again."

"Probably not. But that's no excuse to get involved with an urban terrorist."

"What if—"

She says, "Goodbye, Ryan."

She turns away, starts walking.

He sighs. "Goodbye, Jill."

Chapter 5

Jack cocks his head at a vaguely familiar sound. A voice he hasn't heard since...well, it could be weeks...months...years. Time means nothing when you're chained to a wall in a cell in a basement that's perpetually lit.

There's a group heading down the hall, but the voice belongs to...Bobby. Jack struggles to remember his last name, gives up, listens as the group comes closer.

Jack strains to hear.

Bobby says, "I know this isn't the new life you envisioned, Bill, but don't worry, you're not going to be here very long."

He pauses, then says, "I sold you to the Pinetti brothers. Oh my God, look at your face!"

Then he says, "Wait. Don't be relieved. It's not a joke. I actually *did* sell you to the Pinettis. But don't worry about Alison. I want you to know I'm going to take good care of her. She's a little broad in the beam right now, but that'll change.

You'll be amazed at the difference a month will make in her appearance."

He opens the empty cell across from Jack's. "Alison? This is where you'll be staying. Go on in."

She does.

"Bill?" he says. "I'd like you to meet Jack Tallow. Jack, say hi to Bill."

Jack hisses on cue.

"Jack has been nice enough to donate his cell for the duration of your visit. He and Marcus will be leaving us shortly."

One of Bobby's goons releases Marcus Wisby from his cell, then drags him over, and stands him next to Bill.

Bobby says, "Bill? Do yourself a favor and take a good look at Marcus's private area."

Bill does, and winces.

Bobby says, "That's what'll happen to you if you make a sound louder than a bowel movement during the time you're our guest. Do you understand?"

Bill nods.

Bobby says, "I'm going to test you on that right now, okay?"

He looks at Alison and says, "Remove all your clothes, dear. No, sweetheart, don't look at him. You're mine now. Look at me, and do as I say. Now strip."

Alison starts to cry.

Bobby says, "Do I look like the kind of man who's moved by tears? I'll give you thirty seconds to get naked, or I'll remove your husband's penis with a chain saw."

It takes Alison half the allotted time to get completely naked.

Bobby enters her cell, gathers her clothes, and says, "We'll feed you once a day and remove your shit bucket twice a day. If you spill the bucket, you don't eat that day. Sometimes you'll spill the bucket on purpose, just to break the monotony. We understand it, but you won't want to make a habit of it. Twice a week we'll hose you down, and if you've been cooperative that week, we'll let you use soap. The barber comes in once a week to shave you, including head, underarms, and private area. The first time you make a sound louder than a bowel movement, including crying, I'll have my doctor cut out your vocal cords. That's not a threat, Alison, it's a promise. I know you think I'm a pig, but in time you'll be so lonely for human interaction you'll actually welcome my visits."

Bobby turns to Jack. "How have you been getting along, old sport?"

Jack hisses, and lunges five feet toward the bars, giving Rayburn a perfect opportunity to shoot him with his stun gun. Jack's body lurches as the electrical charge courses through him. Clayton unlocks the cell and gives Jack an injection.

When Jack opens his eyes he laughs. It comes out of his throat as a hiss, but it's loud, and fulfilling. He's laughing for good reason. He may be on his back, his head thick with drugs, but he's outdoors. For the first time since he can remember, he feels the air around him. It's cooler than what he's lived with in Bobby's dungeon, and he detects a light breeze that makes him feel alive.

He laughs again, thinking about how Bobby claimed he'd never see the outdoors again. Well, maybe it's dark, and maybe his hands and legs are hurting like holy hell...

...But Bobby's wrong.

Because Jack's definitely outdoors, and that means he finally beat Bobby DiPiese.

He laughs again.

"What the fuck's he laughin' about?" one of Bobby's goons says from somewhere behind him.

"They all laugh," the other one says. "But that'll end as soon as I let the hogs out."

Jack's mind drifts to a time when a beautiful woman told him her husband kept hogs penned up on the Blood River. He wonders if these are the hogs she was talking about, or if they're descendants.

He can't remember the woman's name...but remembers he loved her.

Chapter 6

Jack had no idea what it would feel like to be eaten by wild hogs, but he certainly didn't think it would feel like this.

Like he's hanging by his feet, swinging in the air.

He expected the high-pitched squealing and deep-throated grunting he's hearing, but...

Wait.

He *is* hanging by his feet, swinging in the air.

The hogs are making furious noises, like they're in the midst of a feeding frenzy...

...But they're below him.

Is he dead? Floating to heaven?

No. Jack's head is fogged with drugs, but he's gradually becoming lucid enough to realize he's hanging upside down, above the hog pen. His ankles are bound with a rope, and there's a hook attached to it, like the kind you'd find at the end of a hoist. The sound of a motor tells Jack he is, in fact, being lifted by a hoist, and it's swinging him up and over the hog fence.

Is he being rescued?

No. Just the opposite. He's being placed in harm's way.

The hoist is lowering him into the penned area where the hogs are feeding with wild abandon.

Feeding on what?

Marcus Wisby, Bobby's former driver.

Jack remembers part of it now. In fact, he remembers a lot more than he did a few minutes ago. Like the woman's name. The one he loved.

Jill DiPiese.

He and Jill planned to run off together, start a new life. They were on the highway, heading to the Baton Rouge airport. Had they followed the plan, stayed on the highway, they might've made it. But like an idiot, Jack deviated from the plan. He let himself get sidetracked by a few live bodies in the trunk of his car. He got off track, off the highway, off the plan...

...And now this.

More recently, he remembers riding in a tow truck with two goons and Marcus Wisby. More accurately, the goons were riding, as he and Wisby had been crammed into the space behind the two seats occupied by the goons. Goon number one, Ray, was driving and telling Gib, the other goon, what to expect, since this was Gib's first trip to the Blood River. At some point they pulled off the road, drove several minutes, came to a stop. The goons dragged Jack and Wisby from the truck, dumped them beside the hog pen.

Jack blacked out.

When he regained consciousness, he assumed they'd already put him in the pen. But the violent hissing he now hears beneath him confirms the goons lowered Wisby into the pen first. And Wisby's arrival in the pen did not go unnoticed by the wild hogs. They're ripping him apart a few feet beneath Jack's head right now, despite Wisby's hisses of protest.

Suddenly the hissing stops, and is replaced by a malignant intestinal odor so vile, so horrific, it exceeds his ability to comprehend.

Perhaps the drugs are helping him cope.

The first-timer goon, the one named Gib, must not be on the same drugs, because when the stench hits his nostrils, Gib vomits like he means it. Vomits so hard, Ray stops operating the hoist, leaving Jack dangling above the chaos in the pen.

"Jesus, Gib!" Ray says. "You're going to hurt the hogs' feelings!"

Between spasms Gib cries, "Oh, God! Oh, God! Oh God!"

Ray says, "Call on someone you know."

"I can't *do* this, Ray. I've got to get out of here!"

Ray laughs and says, "You owe me a beer. No, make that two beers."

"I'll buy you *ten* beers if you get me out of here!"

Gib throws up everything he had in his stomach, then starts puking bile. When that's gone he starts coughing up his spleen.

Ray says, "You never get used to the smell of raw, human intestines, but you adapt. After the third or fourth time your body learns how to control the puke reflex."

"Seriously," Gib says. "I can't do this twice tonight. If they rip the second guy open like that—"

"They will," Ray says, "and when it happens, you'll deal with it."

He goes back to operating the hoist.

Jack remembers hearing them crush Wisby's ankles with a sledge hammer, but for some reason, his ankles were spared. Maybe they got so involved with Wisby they forgot to hobble Jack. Or maybe they each thought the other did it.

Not that it matters much. He's in the pen now, with a half-dozen killer hogs and a life expectancy shorter than Robin Williams's attention span.

Jack feels his head touch dirt, then his shoulders, then his body, as he's lowered to the mucky ground. The hook disengages, then retracts upward.

Ray says, "Wait. You busted his legs, right?"

Gib says, "Who, the second guy?"

"Yeah."

Gib retches again, then says, "Yeah, sure. I busted them while you were opening the gate to let the hogs in. Can we get the fuck out of here now?"

"If you're going to puke all night I'd rather stay here."

"This is the *only* place I'll puke. I swear!"

Ray says, "Think you can handle a titty bar?"

"Oh, hell yeah!"

Jack wants to yell, "Titty bar? Count me in, fellas!" But he can't yell, he can only hiss, and if he did that, the hogs would be on him in seconds. He counts his blessings. For the moment, he's been spared. The hogs are so preoccupied with Wisby, they haven't even noticed him. Yet.

Ray says, "We'll come back in a couple hours, put the pigs back in the other pen, burn the skeletons."

"Why can't they stay in this pen?"

"The pigs?"

"Yeah, why not? It's ten times bigger."

"They'd dig their way out, eventually. The other one's got a six-foot-deep concrete footer around it."

Gib dry heaves one last time. Then says, "Can we fucking go now?"

Chapter 7

Jack's lying in the muck, six feet from the action. One of the hogs pulls a length of intestine from Wisby's torso and slams into Jack's body while trying to make off with it. Another hog clamps his jaws on the other end of the intestine, and the center gives way with a snapping sound that reminds Jack of when he was a senior in high school, snapping wet towels on unsuspecting freshmen's asses in the shower.

Except that snapping asses with towels never caused an explosion of half-digested bowels to fly over a wide area like shit shrapnel.

One of the hogs notices Jack, comes over to check him out. It ruts its snout into Jack's side, bites him savagely, then takes a step back. Whatever reaction it was expecting didn't occur, and its pea-sized brain works overtime to process the result. The hog dives into Jack's torso a second time, rips a baseball-sized hunk of flesh from it, and steps back again, to survey the result. He swallows Jack's flesh nugget, then comes back to lap up the wound.

As excruciating as the pain is, the pig's breath is worse. But Jack forces himself to remain quiet. It's not easy, but he knows his life depends on it.

A flashlight beam suddenly highlights the action.

Ray says, "They found the second guy. He's so drugged up he can't feel a thing."

Gib says, "I almost envy him."

The flashlight hovers on Jack another minute as the hog pushes its snout deeper into the wound, as if seeking a hidden treasure of some sort. An organ, perhaps? A capillary-rich section of subcutaneous fat? Jack has no idea what the human equivalent of a truffle might be, but hopes the hog doesn't find it.

But if it does, Jack's determined not to kick and hiss because he believes his best hope for survival is to employ the same tactic his ex-wife used whenever he felt amorous late at night. He'll remain quiet, refuse to make a sound, or move a muscle. Refuse to give the hog any movement whatsoever. Whatever the hog wishes to do, it can, but there'll be no participation from Jack. And hopefully, the hog will eventually lose interest.

Will it work?

He doesn't know, but it certainly worked for his ex-wife.

When the flashlight moves to Wisby, Gib finds a way to puke again.

Unfortunately for Jack, his rogue hog hasn't lost interest. It gets Jack by the ankle and drags him ten feet further away from the others, licks the wound again, then sneezes into it, and licks it again. Then, just as Jack's about to give up hope, the hog seems to decide that since none of the others are interested in Jack, perhaps it shouldn't be, either. While the others are joyously feasting on the steaming, odorous, open wound that used to be Marcus Wisby's body, Jack's hog is missing out.

The hog pauses another moment, then races to claim its rightful share of the Wisby spoils.

Jack waits till he hears the goons climb into the truck and drive away...

Then he starts rolling toward the far fence.

Chapter 8

Jack's at the fence, but has to find a way to get to his feet and work his hog-bitten body over the top. It would be easier if his ankles weren't bound.

And if he wasn't bleeding profusely.

And if the chain-link fence didn't have two rows of barbed wire above it.

While two strands are better than three, these are pretty high up, and likely to play havoc with Jack's nude, wounded body. Still, the discomfort of the fence pales in comparison to what the hogs have in store for him.

Jack works his way to his feet, puts his left hand on one of the posts, and tries to pull his body upward...

And falls to the ground.

He tries again with the same result, and comes to the conclusion he won't be able to climb the fence with his feet tied. So he sits on the ground and feels around for the knot. Finds it, allows his fingers to explore it in the dark, then hears the unmistakable sound of hoofs coming toward him at a fast clip.

His new friend, the rogue hog, latches onto Jack's ankle and starts pulling him back toward the others. He drags Jack a dozen feet, then stops to get a better grip, and discovers the rope around Jack's ankles. The hog makes quick work of the rope, and Jack's feet are suddenly free. Thinking it's gotten a bit of intestine, the hog runs off to enjoy its prize.

Jack regards this news with mixed emotions. He's happy to be free, but hoped to keep the rope for the new plan he's formulating.

He tells himself not to get distracted by the rope. After all, survival's the first order of business. Jack gets to his wobbly feet and staggers back toward the fence. In an ideal world, he'd try to climb the fence by working his toes into the linked sections and pulling himself up.

But this isn't an ideal world. It's a hog pen filled with wild hogs who suddenly notice Jack trying to climb out of the pen.

They come at him like starving civil war soldiers attacking a stray turkey.

Jack panics and grabs the top section of barbed wire and pulls himself up as fast as he can, scraping long, deep ropes of skin and flesh from his chest in the process.

Though he feels little pain at the moment, he's aware he left a lot of meat on the barbs, and the deep gullies he carved are going to hurt like hell when his adrenalin subsides.

But at least he's still alive.

For the moment.

What he needs to do is get his legs up before the hogs drag him back down.

Although the wire shudders and shakes and affords him very little stability, the hogs snapping at his feet provide all the motivation he needs to swing his right leg up and over the top strand.

Of course, barbed wire's a funny thing. It freely gives, twists, and bends, but when it snaps back in place, it does so with a vengeance. The same springing action that saved him from the hogs moments earlier has now trapped him. His body's hung on the top strand of barbed wire, and his legs are hopelessly entwined in the second strand, and after some pain-filled moments and heartfelt hissing, Jack comes to the realization that regardless of how hard he kicks, or how much he rocks, he's not getting off this fence without help.

With nothing else to do at the moment, he takes inventory as best he can and judges his wounds aren't severe enough to kill him before the goons come back. He also figures if they're sober enough to make it back from the bar, they'll be sober enough to realize there's only one skeleton in the hog pen. Within minutes they'll find him and feed him to the hogs.

So here he remains, stranded atop a barbed-wire fence, stuck between getting away and getting eaten alive. If not for the determination of the hogs, Jack would have about two hours to contemplate how this would be a fitting end, a metaphor for his entire life.

But the hogs are, in fact, determined to get him, and as a result, they begin crashing their bodies into the fence, hoping to dislodge their prey.

And it works.

Jack loses a significant amount of thigh flesh, and his arms and shoulders are raked by the barbed wire, but he crashes to the ground on the safe side of the fence.

He lies there a few minutes, gathering his strength.

As the drugs begin losing their effect, the pain receptors kick in, and Jack begins hissing worse than Marcus Wisby did when his torso was being torn to shreds.

Jack either passes out for a few minutes or thinks he did. It's hard to tell for sure, but the result is the same. He's still in pain, still losing blood, and the hogs are still slamming into the fence, trying to get him.

And Jack still needs to go back in the pen to get one of the ropes. His or Wisby's, whichever one has sustained less damage.

Because his escape plan depends on that rope.

On the bright side, he has an idea how to do it safely, if only the hogs will cooperate.

Chapter 9

Walking on swollen, hog-bitten, barbed wire-scratched legs with gaping wounds in his chest, thigh, side, back, and shoulders, proves more difficult now than before he passed out, thanks to the brief passage of time and the steady erosion of drugs in Jack's system. Not to mention it's practically pitch dark, he's naked, and the terrain on the far side of the pen is littered with roots, pinecones, and the occasional sharp rock.

wJack feels his way around the pen till he gets to the approximate pcint where the goons parked their truck a few minutes ago. The hogs track him step for step from inside the pen. They're angry now, having been denied a golden feeding opportunity.

Jack's happy the hogs are staying close. He knows there's a smaller pen attached to this one, and when he finds the gate, he can lure them in it. Then he'll be able to enter the large pen unmolested, and search for the rope he needs.

It takes ten minutes to find the gates, two more to figure out how they work. Luring the hogs proves easier than expected. Jack opens the gate, the hogs run in. Jack closes it and enters the large pen. He figures his best chance of finding rope is to check the area near Wisby's corpse. Maybe his rope-covered ankles will still be there, or close by.

As it turns out, he's right. Jack finds the rope, and it's still coiled, but weighty. By feeling around, he can tell the feet, ankles and a partial leg bone are still attached to it. He drags the bundle a few yards away from Wisby's remains, hoping to lessen the stink emanating from the kill site, but it all stinks, so he sits in the muck in the dark and starts working on the knot.

As he works, he thinks about how lucky he's been. Bobby didn't cut his balls off. The goons didn't smash his ankles. They didn't put him in the pen first. The barbed wire never cut his face or private area.

A sudden sound tells him he's not alone.

What the fuck?

Jack jumps to his feet, but the hog attacks and rams into him hard enough to send him reeling. When it turns back to come after him again, Jack hears something that gives him hope.

A choking sound.

The hog's choking on something.

A bone?

The hog crashes into Jack again, then stumbles and falls to the ground. It writhes around making gurgling sounds. Its breathing is labored. Just before dying, it squeals a fearsome death cry that sets off a thunderous response from the hogs in the small pen.

Good job, Wisby, Jack thinks. *You choked it to death!*

He unties the rope, drapes it around his shoulders, exits the pen, opens the other gate so the pigs can come back in and eat their former friend. Then he walks to the ditch behind the clearing where the goons will park their truck after returning from the bar.

He lies flat in the ditch and hopes to live long enough to carry out his plan.

Chapter 10

Jack sees the approaching headlights before hearing the truck. As expected, the goons park in the same place, only this time they face the large pen and train their headlights on it. They exit the truck, leaving the lights on, doors open, engine running, so they can hear the country music blasting from the speakers. Before they get ten feet, Jack climbs in the truck, throws it in gear, and mows them down. Then he backs the truck up, gets out, staggers toward the bodies.

Both men are alive, but unable to put up a fight, or mount a defense. Jack finds Gib's gun, stands over him, fires a shot point blank into his forehead. Ray's in decent shape, meaning he's not likely to die anytime soon, but his back appears broken, and he might be paralyzed from the waist down. Jack strips him naked, removes the money and wallet from his pockets, and ties his ankles together with Wisby's rope. Then he gets back in the truck and angles it beside the fence so he can hoist Ray up and over it like Ray hoisted Jack and Wisby a couple hours ago.

If Jack wasn't so drugged and weak from the hog attack and subsequent loss of blood, he'd jump in the truck and hit the highway right now. But in his current state he wouldn't be able to drive a straight line.

What he needs is time. Time to build his strength and let the drugs wear off a little more.

Revenge isn't the motive for hoisting Ray over the hog pen. The reason for doing it is simple.

Jack needs an alarm clock.

Not to wake him, but to keep him from falling asleep.

He needs rest, but not too much. What's the perfect amount?

Something between fifteen and forty-five minutes.

What he *can't* afford is to fall asleep. If he falls asleep he could die from seizure, internal bleeding, trauma, loss of blood, infection, or who knows what else?

So the idea is to hoist Ray up and hang him by his feet over the hog pen. Jack plans to keep him on the hook and bring him to a height that's low enough for the hogs to make contact, but high enough to keep them from killing Ray too quickly.

Ray's screams will keep Jack from falling asleep.

It takes him an inordinate amount of time to get the hoist working properly, and he nearly passes out from the pain of trying to maneuver it. But at last he gets it right, and when Ray shrieks, the hogs listen. They stop feeding on the dead hog and scurry over to see what the live goon has to offer. Jack marvels at the desire these hogs have to continue feeding long after he'd expect them to be satiated.

With Ray in place, Jack lies down on the ground beside the truck and closes his eyes.

Jack was...

He was right.

His body's crying desperately for sleep. Time and again he nods off, but thankfully the hogs never tire of attacking the goon on the hook.

Eventually, the entire truck shakes and groans, as if it's about to topple over. Jack decides it's gone on long enough. Regardless of his ability to drive a straight line, he needs to get out of here. He needs a doctor, or at least some serious antibiotics and a sewing kit.

Wait. Not a doctor. A doctor would send him to the hospital, and the hospital would call the police. Nor would a sewing kit be of much use. Half his wounds will be difficult or impossible for him to reach.

What Jack needs is a veterinarian. A veterinarian could stitch him up and give him drugs.

If he lives long enough to find one.

When Jack climbs into the truck he can practically feel his body raging with infection. He feels the end is near. He sees the gun and knows most people would probably give up. It would be so easy to put the gun barrel in his mouth and pull the trigger. He's got what, four bullets left?

And all he needs is one.

But Jack's not most people. He thinks of all the reasons he has for living. Like seeing Jill again, if she's alive. And if she *is*, he'll want to make sure she's safe.

Of course, he also needs to kill Bobby and the house goons, and free the prisoners in Bobby's basement.

The plan he's formulating to kill one group and free the other is so simple. Bobby and the goons are above ground, the prisoners stay in the basement. The basement is well-built, and those within its walls would almost certainly survive an explosion concentrated on the first floor of Bobby's house. All it would take to create such an explosion is a rocket launcher and three or four warheads similar to the one Bobby claimed Decker was using to blow up Jack's lake house.

Jack takes a moment to wonder if Decker actually bombed the lake house, then decides those thoughts are a distraction to his immediate plan. He sees a newspaper wedged between the console and passenger seat. If he takes the time to look, the paper's date will tell him how long he's been held captive.

He grabs it, then hesitates.

Is he prepared for the answer?

He closes his eyes, takes a deep breath.

What if it's been years?

He lets the breath out slowly.

It hasn't been years.

More likely, it's been six months, eight at the most. It feels like years, but then again, he saw Bobby just hours ago, in the basement, and he didn't appear much older than the day they met.

Jack attacks the paper with confidence, but is startled to learn he's been a prisoner for exactly...

He does the math...

Chapter 11

Four days.

What?

That can't be true. This must be an old paper.

But why would the goons hold on to an old paper?

They wouldn't.

And there's this: a receipt in the cup holder from the bar the goons visited earlier tonight.

Same date.

Okay, so he's only been a prisoner for four days. That's weird, but good, right? It means his vocal cords were removed what, three days ago? Is that possible? And if so, maybe the doctor gave him some antibiotics during the operation that could help him stay alive tonight.

He backs the truck up, cuts the wheels, puts it in gear, and follows the dirt road all the way to the highway, turns right, and does his best not to weave. His immediate plan is to get to Baton Rouge, find a veterinarian who'll sew him up and give him some antibiotics. Then he'll track Decker down and score the munitions necessary to blow up Bobby's house. If it turns out Decker killed Jill, he'll kill him after getting the weapons.

What if he can't find Decker?

What? Can't find *Decker*? Is he *serious*? Where did *that* thought come from? Jack would laugh out loud if he could. Of *course* he'll find Decker! Finding people is what he does best. But if he can't find Decker in the next twenty-four hours he'll have to score the munitions from someone else, because it won't take long for Bobby to find out Jack's alive.

So what's the plan?

It's...um...uh....blow up Bobby's house, haul ass, and leave it to the cops to sift through the rubble, find the prisoners, and set them free. Then he'll find out if Jill's dead. If she is, he'll find Decker and kill him. If she's alive, he'll ask if she can find it in her heart to give him another chance.

Even though he's lost his voice. Even though his body will look like a jigsaw puzzle when the vet finishes stitching him up. Even though...

Jack's distracted by the car coming up behind him at breakneck speed. Within seconds it pulls up beside him, adjusts to Jack's speed. The passenger window goes down, and a stoner dude points behind Jack's truck.

Jack waves.

The stoner car honks twice, and roars off like a scalded owl.

Thirty seconds pass as Jack watches the car become a small red dot on the horizon. Then he checks his rearview mirror and sees nothing. Not that he expected to. After all, it's the wee hours of the morning, and pitch black out here, in the middle of nowhere.

Jack touches the brake pedal lightly, to illuminate the area behind him, and is surprised to see the bottom half of a man's torso hanging from the hoist.

He slows down some more, to get a better look at what's left of Ray, the naked goon, who's flapping in the breeze.

For a minute he thinks about taking the next exit and getting the fuck off the highway. But then he remembers what happened the last time he did that. He wound up smack in the middle of the Virgin Boat Festival. That was what, five days ago?

Something like that.

And look at all that's happened since!

Jack decides to pull a FIDO, which stands for *Fuck it, drive on!*

After a few minutes Jack passes an exit and wonders if maybe he should at least pull over and dump the body on the side of the road. Wouldn't that be the sensible thing to do?

No.

Because every time he deviates from a plan he takes a step backward. He planned to not sleep with the local girls in Willow Lake. He planned to not fall in love with Jill. He planned to take her straight to Bobby's house. He deviated from all those plans, and look what happened.

Wait, did he think that already?

Enough.

This time, no deviation. Jack will stick to the plan, which is...which is...to drive straight to Baton Rouge. Yeah, that's right. He'll drive to Baton Rouge, where he'll find a vet to sew him up and give him drugs. Then he'll score munitions to blow up Bobby's house. Then he'll kill Bobby and the goons and help free the prisoners. Then he'll find out if Jill's alive. If so, he'll try to talk her into living with him.

Except that he can't talk.

No problem. He'll learn sign language. But will she?

Probably not. So big deal, he'll have to find a way to communicate. That's fine, he'll figure something out.

The key is to make a plan and stick to it.

He taps the brake and watches Ray swing in the breeze.

Jack's fully aware some people might think he's taking a chance by driving on the highway or through the streets of Baton Rouge with half a blood-soaked, leaking, naked torso hanging from a hook behind his tow truck. But Jack's always been more of a "glass half-full" kind of guy.

An optimist.

He'll stick to his plan. It's a good one. A sound one.

And anyway, he's made it this far, hasn't he? After all he's been through, what're the chances something could possibly go wrong?

THE END

Personal Message from John Locke:

I love writing books! But what I love even more is hearing from readers. If you enjoyed this or any of my other books, it would mean the world to me if you'd send a short email to introduce yourself and say hi. I always personally respond to my readers.

I would also love to put you on my mailing list to receive notifications about future books, updates, and contests.

Please visit my website:

http://www.DonovanCreed.com

John Locke

New York Times Best Selling Author

8th Member of the Kindle Million Sales Club
(Other members: Stieg Larsson, James Patterson, Nora Roberts,
Charlaine Harris, Lee Child, Suzanne Collins, Michael Connelly)

First self-published author to hit #1 on Amazon/Kindle!

First self-published author to hit Kindle Million Sales Club!

Sold 1,100,000 eBooks in 5 months through word of mouth!

Wrote and published 6 best-selling books
in 3 separate genres in 6 months!

Had 4 of the top 10 eBooks on Amazon/Kindle at the same time,
including #1 and #2!

Had 6 of the top 20, and 8 books in the top 43 at the same time!

John Locke has written 17 books in three years, all best-sellers!

John Locke

New York Times Best Selling Author
#1 Best Selling Author on Amazon Kindle

Donovan Creed Series:
Lethal People
Lethal Experiment
Saving Rachel
Now & Then
Wish List
A Girl Like You
Vegas Moon
The Love You Crave
Maybe
Callie's Last Dance

Emmett Love Series:
Follow the Stone
Don't Poke the Bear
Emmett & Gentry

Dani Ripper Series:
Call Me!
Promise You Won't Tell?

Dr. Gideon Box Series:
Bad Doctor
Box

Other:
Kill Jill

Non-Fiction:
How I Sold 1 Million eBooks in 5 Months!